Complicit Witness

Complicit Witness

Dan Petrosini

Copyright © Dan Petrosini 2013
All rights reserved. No part of this publication may be reproduced, stored in a retrieval system, or transmitted, in any form or by any means, electronic, mechanical, photocopying, recording or otherwise, without the prior written permission of the publishers.

The novel is entirely a work of fiction Any resemblance to actual persons, living or dead, is entirely coincidental. For requests, information, and more, contact Dan Petrosini at dan@danpetrosini.com

Available in ebook and print.

ISBN-13: 978-1491095614

ISBN-10: 149109561X

Other Books by Dan

Luca Mystery Series

Am I the Killer—Book 1
Vanished—Book 2
The Serenity Murder—Book 3
Third Chances—Book 4
A Cold, Hard Case—Book 5
Cop or Killer?—Book 6
Silencing Salter—Book 7
A Killer Missteps—Book 8
Uncertain Stakes—Book 9
The Grandpa Killer—Book 10
Dangerous Revenge—Book 11
Where Are They—Book 12

Suspenseful Secrets

Cory's Dilemma—Book 1

Other works by Dan Petrosini

The Final Enemy
Complicit Witness
Push Back
Ambition Cliff

Acknowledgments

Special thanks to Julie, Stephanie and Jennifer for their love and support.

Dedicated to the lifelong friends and characters met on Staten Island.

Chapter One

With a few more miles to go and dusk descending into darkness, I was getting antsy.

There were only two cars in the lot, and I parked in the dark by the loading dock. I checked the time and pulled a dry bagel and can of Coke out of the cooler. I took a bite but craved a meatball sandwich, anything but another damn bagel. I shrunk down as a car drove out of the lot and then guzzled some soda.

Checking the rearview mirror, I pulled a bag from under the seat and stepped out into the humidity. As the gravel crunched underfoot, I finished the soda and tossed the can into the woods as I climbed a set of stairs to a door.

Surveying the lot, I pushed open the door and walked into a foyer caged in by a chain-link barrier.

Peering through the fence I tried the handle, then shook the fencing. "Yo Rick!"

My reed-thin contact popped out of a side room, "Great, you're early." He hurried to open the gate.

"Yeah, no traffic for a change, flew straight down."

"Works for me. Emily wants to go the pictures tonight."

Pictures? These fucking hicks were frozen in time. We went into a small room that featured a smiling picture of President Carter. I emptied the bag on the table, stacking the rubber-banded bundles of hundreds into neat rows, four high.

Rick fanned a few of the bundles. "One, two, three, four…"

"It's all there, Mayberry, forty thou," I said, lighting a cigarette.

He lifted an eyebrow at the hillbilly reference but kept counting.

"Always nice doing business with you city slickers," Rick said, loading the cash into a satchel. "You stay put. I'm gonna put this in the safe."

"How much you got in that safe?"

"Sonny boy, ya know I can't tell ya. Besides, it's cleaned out every night."

I smiled broadly. "Yeah, what time you do that?"

He shook his head. "You really something, kid."

We walked to the back of the warehouse where Rick rolled up the loading dock door where I always parked.

"Rick, hang on a minute. I gotta take a leak."

"Go on, I'll get started."

I drained my bladder the best I could, doing knee bends to help empty it and hurried back.

As we finished loading the cargo I heard a dog's bark that seemed to be silenced too quickly.

"What the hell was that?"

"It's nothing."

I looked around. "You sure?"

"Just a wild dog, that's all. Okay, that does it."

I unfurled a bedsheet, adjusting it to cover my cargo.

"Okay, Rick, I'll see your skinny ass next week, same time, same place, bro."

"Fer sure, Thomas. Be careful, young man."

"Don't worry about me, bro. I got it down to a science."

I stretched my hamstrings and thighs and jumped behind the wheel as the hick rolled down the door. This is getting really old, I thought, as I popped an upper. I wished Jackpot was around for company as I shot gravel on the way out of the lot. I really missed her; she'd sit on my lap and lick my hand as I drove.

Images of her at the vet looking at me crept into my head, and I turned up the air-conditioning to change the mood, hoping that Grease would be ready to make trips in a few weeks. A smile spread when I thought about how nuts she'd go when I got home.

Hitting the ramp for the interstate, I hunted among the country radio stations for a disco channel to distract me during the drive. Before I passed the first exit, my mind drifted to the chick I'd met at the vet.

When Jackpot's heart condition worsened I rushed her to Boulevard Veterinary on Hylan. She could hardly breathe, hoarsely coughing as I carried her into the empty office.

"Hi, may I help you?"

"She can't breathe. She's hacking away, not eating, not doing anything but lying around."

"Has she been here before? What's the name?"

"She's in trouble; I'm telling you. You got to hurry."

"Okay, take it easy, we'll do what we can. Follow me."

We went into a stark room with an exam table and a sink with a hose contraption.

"Let's put her on the table, and I'll get the doctor."

I put her down and she shook, peeing on the table.

"She's nervous. Let me hold her. She'll be okay."

"Sure, make her comfortable." She stroked Jackpot as I held her. "Good girl; you'll be okay. Daddy has you now." Jackpot attempted to lick her hand.

"She likes you. What's your name?"

"Donna."

"See, Jackpot, calm down. Donna's gonna get the doc, and we'll see what's going on."

A tall man in a lab coat and clogs swung open the door.

"What symptoms has the dog had?"

I explained her history of heart congestion and that she had stopped eating yesterday. Jackpot was whimpering and wheezing as he examined her, putting a stethoscope to her chest.

"It doesn't sound good. There is a lot of fluid in her chest cavity. Let's get an X-ray." He picked her up and Jackpot cried.

"Doc, gimme her. She's scared."

"That's all right. I'll take her." Donna caressed Jackpot, who quieted down immediately. She smiled, and I finally noticed how good looking she was.

The vet came out, telling me she didn't have long to live. I was pissed; he was a coldhearted bastard, suggesting I should put her down.

"No way, man."

"She's suffering."

"Can't you give her something?"

Donna jumped in. "Sometimes you can use a diuretic? Right, Doc?"

"We can give her some. It will help to reduce the fluids, but it's not a cure. Just a temporary measure. You really should consider putting her out of her misery."

"How long will she feel better?"

"It's not an exact science; her condition is degenerative. You'll be back with her, guaranteed."

The medicines worked for three weeks, but that bastard was right, I thought, as I headed north with my load.

Chapter Two

The sun had been up for a couple of hours as I cruised down Forest Avenue, passing the Hess Station. A sale sign was on a tower of oil cans, giving me the all-clear signal.

I made a U-turn into the station, brushed my hair and hopped out. "Hey, bro, top it off, high test." I pulled out my BIC lighter, lit a cigarette and walked to the back of the building.

After straightening my shirt, I gave the door three rapid knocks, and it swung open. Tony scanned the area.

"Hey, kid, any trouble?"

"Nah."

"Good, let's move it."

I hopped back in the car and pulled under an opening garage door.

The door slammed shut behind me, and three goons quickly began unloading my cargo, spreading the contents into two cars that pulled out of the garage before I got out of the bathroom.

I lit another smoke. "Where's my unc?"

"Lou's not in yet."

Uncle Louie wasn't really my uncle; he was my mom's cousin, but I grew up calling him uncle. "Still home?"

"Yeah, the boss wasn't feeling too good, sore throat or something."

The Bagel Express truck was being worked on. "Getting the van ready?"

"Yeah, changing the oil and plugs."

"Isn't it early?"

"Yeah, Josephine called said they may be going down, and you know how he's gotta have his bread."

I nodded. I really did know. I loved my bread and had to hand it to Louie; he found a way to get fresh Brooklyn bread a couple of times a week and make a few bucks along the way by supplying stores near his Boca Raton home.

"What about my dough?"

"Angie's got it. He's in the back."

"Hope he didn't eat it."

"Watch yourself, Tommy; one day you're gonna get it."

"What's he gonna do? Sit on me?" I snickered as I nodded to one of new faces around. "This Russian seems like he's always around now."

"Yeah, the boss and Yuri doing more business together."

I headed to get my pay for the run from Angelo, who was really fat and slicked his jet-black hair back with enough gel to grease an engine. He was at a round table reading a newspaper whose headline shouted the capture of the killer, Son of Sam.

"Yo, Tubby, you got something for me?"

He fingered a bat leaning against the table. "Yeah, right here, you little bastard."

"Temper, temper, tubs."

He got up as quickly as I ever saw him move, and as I backed up, he broke into an evil smile. "Ya just a fuckin' mouthpiece, you little punk."

He waddled over to my uncle's desk and dug out an envelope.

"Come and get it, wiseguy." He held the envelope against his protruding belly, and as I reached for it he grabbed my wrist.

"Let go, you fucking ape!"

"One of these days, kid." He tossed the envelope on the ground and I scooped it up.

"Adios, you fat bastard."

I counted twenty crisp one-hundred-dollar bills.

"Hey, this is light! You step on it?"

"I should've, punk; the boss took five out to knock your tab down."

"That's fucking bullshit, man!"

"Go cry to Louie, you degenerate."

Chapter Three

Tuesday nights were a sort of mini reunion. The four of us enjoyed the bowling and comradeship, trading stories in between a serious gambit to win the league and side bets made during the night.

We had a strong team: Larry aka Red, Phil nicknamed Felix and Mark the Spark. All with averages in the high one eighties, we were a force each year to win the four thousand dollar first-place prize and bragging rights. No one drank anything hard until we finished our matches. We were in the last game of the set and were up a hair.

"Yo, Red, you're up."

"Philly, you see Tommy last night?"

"Nah, he's been holing up with that girl Donna."

"Donnarrhea? Again?"

"You mean he's back with that bitch that gave him the clap?"

"Nah, same name, different panties," Red said from the approach, ready to deliver.

The pins exploded, and we jumped up, high-fiving each other.

"Nice, Red. Keep it going, Vince!"

I threw a spare, and we went on to win the match, hanging on to our first-place ranking. We settled up our side bets and retreated to the bar for a drink.

"Tommy stopping by?"

"I donno. He's hot and heavy with Donna."

"Yeah right, till the next one comes along."

"Or till she gets fed up with his bullshit," Red said as he lit a smoke.

"It'd be good if he settled down a bit. He needs something to ground him." I offered.

"Ground him? I'm beginning to lose faith. Sparko, did you hear what he did to Red?" Phil was already laughing as he continued, "We were at Henny's, catching lunch; Joey was working the bar, so the booze was flowing. Red got frigging ossified."

"You could never hold your booze, Red."

"Bullshit, man. I was dead tired; we put in two pools while you pussies were still in bed."

"Yeah, yeah."

"Anyway, the place starts to empty out, and one of the Mexicans in the back says he smells gas. Con Ed comes down, and we head to the parking lot. Red lies on the hood of Tommy's car, and in fifteen he's snoring like fucking Rip Van Winkle. Skins sneaks behind the wheel and waves us in. He starts it up and slams it into drive as Red wakes up. Red rolls over on his belly, grabbing the hood as Tommy hits the gas."

"Something really wrong with this guy." Mark shakes his head.

"It was so funny. I know it's sick, but you gotta picture Red, staring through the windshield, screaming his ass off."

"Yeah, real funny when you're hanging on for your fucking life."

"Then the nut pulls onto Richmond Avenue."

"Ah, come on!"

"I swear. He goes to the first light and cuts off onto Rockland and takes the back streets all the way to Hylan."

"My fucking hands nearly gave out."

"You sobered up though." Phil laughed.

Sparko shook his head. "It's no joke. One day someone's gonna get hurt."

I met Tommy a few weeks after moving to the Island. Riding bikes with a friend, Tommy was walking on Arlene Street with a sack full of brown packages. My first impression was he had a square head and was straight out of Brooklyn. An amazing observation, not for the boxy head but the fact I'd moved from Brooklyn a month before. We asked him if he was going to play ball, but he had to help his dad. We rode off to our game.

We were about twelve years old and quickly formed a group who loved to play ball, bust each other's chops and torment people with our pranks. Tommy was a world-class ball buster and a virtual nickname machine.

You either loved him or hated him. Most loved him in spite of an underlying acidity that would break out into pure nastiness at times.

After the day's games were over we hung around at the edge of the woods on a heap of asphalt we named The Elephant. After rehashing the day's match, we'd quickly revert to ragging on someone and making jokes as dinnertime rolled around. A few guys, including Tommy, whose family had an unconventional twist to it, stayed as I headed home. We had a standing rule; the family ate together each and every night, no ifs, ands or buts about it. My dad was old school and hard working. He was home every night and certainly wasn't flashy like a lot of dads in the neighborhood. It was a memorable time that went by in a flash.

As we hit our late teens, Tommy always seemed to have money to blow on gambling, booze and drugs. Guess he picked up the habit from his father who was always in a bar chasing broads or at the racetrack, and depending on how his fortunes were doing at the time, even owned a couple of horses.

The ultimate good-time Charley, Tommy loved a good time, and as we grew older, seriously overdid the partying. He always would push things past their natural limits. He'd bust balls or irritate someone past the point of no return, and a fight would break out. Funny thing was, when the fighting broke out he was nowhere to be found.

He was like a midlevel glass of scotch, a little burn, but if you went for more, felt better in the end. However, if you had too much, the hangover could be painful.

Chapter Four

Tommy had an uncle named Louie, or so I thought. Lou had a bar among other moneymaking enterprises and "ran" things on Staten Island. I eventually realized he was the source of income for quite of few of the families in my middle-class neighborhood. Now, they were easy to spot, fathers around during the day, hanging in the diner, going the track, driving Lincolns or big Chryslers. They were on the cusp of flashy but never living too large.

    The houses in the neighborhood were all cookie-cutter from the curb, but the homes of those in the Louie loop were markedly different on the inside. The latest electronic gear and gaudiest furnishings you could imagine were crammed into every room. There was an unspoken contest they seemed to enjoy playing: trying to outdo each other while not running afoul of the Louie Low-Key Rule. Louie was adamant about attracting attention, a tough thing for these bulls, and would admonish anyone showy.

    Two short car horn beeps, and I looked out to confirm it was Tommy. We were heading to a bar, Louie had a piece of, to hang with some girls we met on Friday night. I said goodbye, ran down the stairs into a muggy summer night and hopped in his new Thunderbird.

    "Take it easy on the cologne, Skins." I'd been calling him Skins as he'd been shedding his shirt at places other than a basketball court.

    "Is it too much?"

    I opened the window. "Just a tad, Romeo. Before we get a chance to charm 'em they might pass out."

"Very funny, Otis." He called me Otis, after the elevator company, as I started a job in a Manhattan office building. I had to admit he was a clever bastard.

"I gotta stop to see my Unc first."

The block was mobbed, no pun intended, with cars, but the driveway empty.

"Leave the radio on."

After fifteen minutes, Tommy came out saying he had to stay; his uncle wanted him to eat. I said I'd walk back to my house, but he insisted I stay with him. As we walked toward the back, a guy with a gleaming head and a neck like a bull, grunted at Tommy as he brushed by.

"Who's Mister Personality?"

"A Russian from Brooklyn got a steady line of swag for Louie."

The house seemed ordinary, but when we walked through the yard's gate, I was thrown for a loop. The side yard was a vegetable garden, replete with tomato and basil plants, but the backyard was a resort. A black-bottomed, free-form pool dominated the yard, which was filled with statues and lush landscaping. Flagstone patios accommodated the seating areas which were crammed with guests.

I could see his uncle holding court at the largest table as we talked with his aunt. We made up dishes of food and were about to sit when his cousin Butch said his uncle wanted us. We carried our plates over as a Jerry Vale record played.

"Hey, Unc. This is Vinny; he lives on Dawson."

He suppressed a cough. "Johnnie's boy, right?" Before I could answer, he said, "Pauly, Frank, get up. I want to talk to my nephew. Sit down, boys."

We took their seats and he said that he knew my father, a good guy, he said making me comfortable. I was conscious of how I ate, which was crazy given others were eating like pigs. The surreal setting was about to get elevated when Louie's wife came over,

"Joey, don't Tommy look good in a moustache?"

I was thrown when Uncle Louie said, "Yeah, looks just like his grandpa."

"You were his fav, Joey."

"That fucking cancer took him too early."

Joey, Louie? What was his name?

We ate, talked about the Yankees, the hot weather we were having and the trip to Italy he was looking forward to. He seemed like a nice guy, unlike his reputation. Desserts and black coffee were coming out of the house, and Tommy smelled an opening to break loose.

"Unc, we gotta go."

"Stay for the pastries; they're from Livotti's."

"Love to, but you see, we met these girls and…"

He struggled to clear his throat. "Don't get too close till you really know them. Understand?"

"Of course, Unc. We just want to have a good time."

"Josephine, get the boys a couple pastries to take with them."

He cranked up a Donna Summer tune as we pulled out of the driveway.

"What's up with your aunt calling your uncle, Joey?" I took a bite of cannoli.

"That's his real name. The guys on the street call him Louie."

You know what? Weird as it was, it fit, and I didn't give it another thought.

"The cannoli's good, but man, I'm stuffed. Hey, what was that other girl's name again?"

"Charlene."

"Oh yeah," Tommy said as he sped down the exit ramp. "You think you'll get anywhere with her?"

"I dunno. I think I got a shot."

He lit a cigarette, and I rolled down the window.

"Crank that up. My hair's gonna get messed."

"You got enough hairspray in it to stand up to a jet engine."

He made a left turn into a busy parking lot.

"Is that them?"

"Yup, looking pretty hot, bro."

"Grab me two packs out of the glove." He pulled into a spot.

"Here, give me the keys."

"Okay, Daddy. Let's go."

Louie and his gang ran their enterprise primarily from two places, a tavern and a gas station. Cue Shot was a popular place with a huge bar and pool tables. Known for its brick-oven pizza and Italian male patrons, it was always packed. It did a brisk takeout business, providing good cover for Louie, who was technically a partner. Louie acquired his stake when the owner borrowed to expand and compounded the error by gambling to try to make the money back.

The Hess gas station was another revelation. Hess stations usually only sold gas, doing no auto repairs. They never had a garage or building other than a glass cubicle for the attendant. That is, unless it was Louie's place. At his Hess station, the attendants' glass enclosure wasn't on an island in the middle of the pumps but was at the back end of the station. A door in the enclosure, marked Employees Only, led to a cavernous warehouse.

The warehouse's cement floor was always neatly stacked with a revolving assortment of boxes. In the far corner was a big wooden desk sitting on a large area rug and bunch of folding chairs around two circular tables. The opposite corner was outfitted with a full kitchen, stove, fridge, everything.

The first time I visited the station, Tommy's uncle was behind the desk stacking cash as it shot out of the money counter. He saw us, told one of his minions to clear the dough off the desk, and waved us over.

Louie took his cigar out of his mouth to kiss his nephew, and I awkwardly stuck my hand out,

"How are you doing, Uncle Louie?" I had thought about what to call him on the way there and thought Mr. Ruffino seemed too formal and Louie too personal.

"Nice to see you again. You watching out for my nephew?"

Before I could answer, he said, "This here is Gene and Frankie, and that's Jimmy."

We said our hellos and Tommy asked, "Hey, Unc, the new kid pumping, what's he, a fucking Arab?"

"Egyptian. None of the kids from the neighborhood wanna work anymore; they think pumping gas is beneath them. They don't know what work is."

"Frigging prima donnas they are." Gene, a slender, well-dressed associate added.

"Frankie, close out the pumps and do a count."

Usually done at the end of a shift, closing out the pumps was simply a reading of how much gas was pumped and how much money should have been collected. Louie was seated behind the desk with Gene in a side chair. Tommy and I were sitting ten feet away at the kitchen table when Frankie marched in Wael, the gas attendant.

"Boss, the kid's short fifty."

"You sure, Frankie?"

"Checked it twice."

"Wael, you take the fifty?"

"No, no, no way, Mr. Ruffino."

"You sure you didn't take it?"

"I swear,. I swear!"

Gene said, "Give me the pump readings."

Frankie read off four numbers, and Gene asked, "You check the readings with Frankie, Wael?"

"Yes, yes, they are correct."

Gene plugged the numbers in a calculator. "So you should have twelve hundred and seventy."

"Well, Wael here only had twelve hundred twenty."

"Empty your pockets, you thief," Gene demanded.

The kid spilled the contents of his pockets onto the desk. Besides loose change and keys he only had eleven dollars.

"Where'd you hide the money, Wael?"

The attendant had sweat beading on his upper lip. "I, I didn't. I didn't take anything."

"You know what we do with thieves? We cut their God damn fingers off!"

The kid put his hand on the desk for support, and when Frankie grabbed it, his knees buckled.

"Whaddya want to do with him, boss?"

Louie eyed the kid for a minute and reached into a drawer, coming up with an ax.

The gas attendant screamed, and everyone broke into laughter. Frankie let the kid go and he ran for it. Tony stepped in front the door as Frankie yelled, "Hey, kid, we're only fucking with you. Get over here."

Tony walked him back and Louie said, "Listen kid, you didn't take my money, and I want to be sure you don't ever think about it. You understand?"

"I, I, yes. Sure, Mr. Ruffino. I'd never do that."

Louie coughed as he peeled a fifty off his wad.

"Now take this, and get back to work."

As the door to the station closed they joked, "You see that fucking Arab? He nearly shit his pants."

"I thought fucking Frankie was gonna have to prop his ass up!"

"Yeah, this was better than the time with that skinny kid; what's his name?"

I didn't want to let on that I was as spooked as the kid was. In a way it was kind of funny, but these guys were twisted.

Chapter Five

Yuri bounded up the stairs of St. John's Orthodox Church and pushed open its massive iron doors. The church was empty, and after lighting a candle he settled into a front pew. He prayed for the souls of his parents, and his mind drifted to his humble upbringing in a Moscow suburb. He recalled his father taking him to St. Paul's as a little boy, passing the faith to him. Yuri enjoyed spending the Sundays with his dad in the mysterious surroundings of the ornate church, but as he grew older, he'd rather play in the alleys than go to Mass, and as a teenager stopped going entirely.

As Yuri hit his midthirties the pull of faith and tradition drove him back to church, albeit under a cloud of hypocrisy. Arriving in Brooklyn he bounced around churches until he met Father George, pastor of St. Peter's. Father George wasn't judgmental and never pushed Yuri even though the rumors of his livelihood were hard to ignore. It was a symbiotic relationship; Father George enjoying the donations and Yuri seeking cleansing and dispensation.

Yuri fought to maintain concentration, staring at an icon of Mother Mary as he fingered Rosary beads, when the vestibule door creaked open.

"Ah, Yuri, you're here early."

"Want to do my prayers, Padre."

"Good. That's important, Yuri. You know it doesn't matter what you or anyone does; we can receive forgiveness from God. But we have to mean it, son."

Yuri ran his hand over his gleaming head. "How's it going? Soup kitchen full?"

"Yes, thanks to you, son."

"Good, now what this St. Vincent Paul?"

Father George explained that the organization ministered the poor, helping with rent, utilities and other necessities for those who'd been stressed by the bad economy. Yuri, getting more details than he cared to hear, reached into his jacket and pulled out a brown paper bag.

"Take. I gotta go."

"I don't know what this parish would do without you, Yuri."

Yuri was part of a flood of Russians who fled a crumbling Soviet Union. With the Russian economy forcing many to rely on their wits to survive, Yuri hustled as a teenager to help his parents. When they both fell sick and died he moved into a small, dingy apartment with an uncle. Living a meager existence, Yuri was looking for an exit plan when he heard about the American Jewish Federation who ran an operation relocating Jews to America. He wasn't Jewish, but he paid a bribe and hopped on a ship to America.

Yuri settled in Brighton Beach, an area of Brooklyn dominated by the Russian Jewish community, and worked as busboy in a busy deli to pay his share of the rent. Living in a cramped apartment with five people whose backgrounds differed was tolerable only because of the working hours he put in to survive. Any spare time was used playing soccer in a Russian league, where he met a couple of young Commie toughies who made their money working for the rising Russian mob.

After a year of carousing with the young hoods, Yuri was making pocket money helping with running the numbers game. He also accumulated three tattoos and shaved his head to emulate the menacing look of his hero, heavyweight boxing champ Viktor Ribakov.

With a taste of the street's easy money, Yuri ditched the notion of assimilating for three hundred bucks a week running numbers for the local boss Sergei.

He performed well for Sergei; expanding into the high schools and ensuring all debts were promptly paid. After two years, he was rewarded with running most of the Russian mob's Brooklyn gambling activities. Yuri was as ruthless as his bosses, breaking bones when payments were slow and built loyalties with his men by spreading cash around when they helped him. However, he was just one of a handful of young underlings until a habitual gambler got into trouble.

The bettor had a bad streak of luck and couldn't pay his debts. Yuri knew the guy worked in a warehouse at Bush Terminals, beneath the Gowanus. He and his goons threw a soft beating on him, and when they smelled his fear, told him if he wanted to survive he'd have to work his debt off by providing details on what products were hauled into the warehouse.

The swag business turned into a steady stream of income for Sergei who rewarded Yuri with more power and territory. It kept Yuri satisfied until a mixup in trucks presented an opportunity that crossed paths with the Staten Island Italians.

Yuri got a tip on a truck carrying perfumes and hijacked it as it sat at a red light under the Gowanus. When they opened the truck, inside a Greenpoint warehouse, they found it was loaded with a hundred thousand cartons of Marlboros. With no quick way to lay off the smokes, Yuri and Sergei decided to approach the Ruffino crew who had established a significant cigarette operation. They struck a deal to fence the smokes to Louie's gang, and though at a disadvantage, the money they split was better than usual.

Yuri smelled opportunity, and as he worked out the details of his latest scheme, he kept closer contact with Louie's gang, fencing more goods through them to build trust.

While the Italians had a pipeline to bring their smokes up north, Yuri was bolder. He began to regularly hijack truckloads of cigarettes and sold them at very low prices.

As the market began to collapse the Italians quickly learned that Yuri was undercutting them. A sit-down ensued with the goal of shutting him down, but when Yuri told them of his setup and the drastically lower prices he had, the threat took a back seat to greed, and a partnership was born. Yuri would be a low-price, high-volume source of smokes they'd combine with their pipeline. The lower-blended costs and additional supply would allow for expanded distribution.

Chapter Six

Sundays you never saw Tommy. We thought he was shaking off the partying from the weekend. It made sense; we all stayed in bed Sundays as Mom's gravy wafted in the air. We'd eat like animals, watch whatever games were on and get ready for clubbing that night. However, Tommy never made it out on Sundays and you couldn't reach him at home. We believed he was paying the price for over doing it; make that, way over doing the drinking, coke, ludes and whatever else he consumed.

He wasn't around much in the early part of the week, claiming he was occupied with his dad. As time went by he began to confide in me, believing I'd offer sound advice and keep it confidential.

On Friday I had gotten tickets for the Yanks World Series game for Sunday night. Tommy was huge Yankee fan and I expected a whooping response. Hopping into his smoke-filled car, I cranked a window open as he pulled away. A Bee Gees was blaring and I lowered the volume,

"It's your lucky day, bro!"

"You gotta tip?"

"Better than that." I waved the tickets in front of his face. "Sunday night, Yankee Stadium.. A little game is going on, and we're gonna be there!"

He drew on a cigarette and exhaled slowly. "Can't make it, man."

"What? It's the World Series."

"No can do. Close that window. My hair's gonna get fucked up."

"Yo, Skins, it's those seats on the dugout, man. It's gonna be unreal."

He was stone faced. Puzzled, I pushed.

"You're joking, right? You want me to ask Red?"

"Hey, man, believe me. I fuckin' wanna go, but I got shit to do."

"What the heck you gotta do that can't wait till Monday?"

He flicked his cigarette butt out the window, "Listen, what you think I do every Sunday?"

"The way you party? Nursing a serious hangover!"

He snickered. "Yeah, that too, but I've been helping my old man out."

I didn't say anything as it confirmed he was up to something.

"Anyway, change the fucking subject. I'll tell you about it sometime."

"No prob, bro. Whenever you're ready. Just do me a favor and watch your ass."

"Yeah, and do me a favor; don't invite Red. He's a Mets fan!"

We headed to Port Richmond's outdoor basketball courts where we'd been playing in round robin tournaments since junior high. Though no one on our team was close to six feet, we could all shoot the shit out of the hoop and were competitive.

"Nice game, Spence."

"Spence?"

"Yeah, you were chucking the three pointers like Spencer Hayward!"

Now I could look forward to being called Spence for a few weeks. "I thought that kid wasn't getting back up. Man, he hit hard."

"Yeah, well, I gave him a little help on the way down." He opened his trunk and flipped the lid on a cooler.

I grabbed a juice, but Tommy popped a beer and took a long draw.

"How the hell you drink that now?"

He belched. "Beer really quenches your thirst; you should try it."

"Is Joey back from Boca?"

"Supposed to get in later."

"Good, he was at Uncle Sam's when we met those broads from Islip. They said they're coming to the Island tonight. Told them we'd meet them at Hadar; it's the closest to the bridge for them."

"You're a real Goody Two-shoes, Spence!"

"Come on, let's hit the road. I wanna shower and get ready."

"Yeah, I'm going to get my nails done and walk Grease."

Like a lot of the street guys, Tommy always had his fingernails manicured and polished with a low gloss, an attempt at distancing themselves from how they earned a buck.

"How she doing with the training?"

"Almost there. She's really something. She listens to me."

Tommy made a U-turn across the double line into a Shell station. "I gotta gas up."

The attendant came over. "What's it gonna be?"

"Fill it: high test."

After a minute or so another car pulled into the station, and Tommy said, "How much the pump say?"

"Twenty bucks and change."

Tommy looked over at the attendant getting orders from the other car, put the car in drive and screeched away.

"What the hell are you doing, man?"

I looked back, and the gas pump was spewing gas as we pulled away.

"Holy shit! You're fucking nuts; you know that?"

Tommy had a big grin on his face. "That towel head don't know what hit him."

"You're crazy, you know. One of these days you're going to get arrested."

He burst out laughing and I joined in.

You just never knew what the day would bring with him. It made it fun, but the second thoughts were getting more prominent with every episode. Tommy had no apparent limits, and I knew one day he wouldn't be able to walk on water. I just had to be sure I wasn't in drowning distance.

Another U-turn. "Where you going now?"

"That's Rocco's, Tess's favorite bakery; I wanna pick up some sesame cookies for her."

Tommy had a weird habit of calling his mother by her first name. I considered it disrespectful and always called her Mrs. A. I don't know when it started, but it had to originate with his father who seemed to despise his wife.

He pulled up to my house.

"What time you want me to pick you up?"

"Uhm, I'll meet you there around ten. I, uh, got to take a ride with my dad." I had to make sure I took my own car.

Chapter Seven

"Vinny, is that for you?"

I looked through the window. It was Tommy who had beeped the horn. "Yeah, Mom, I got it."

Tommy leaned on the horn again as I bounded down the stairs. I could hear Barry White crooning away as I trotted to the car. "Geez, take it easy. The whole frigging neighborhood is looking out the window."

"Jump in. You got money?"

"Ah, a hundred and change. Whats up?"

"I'll lend you some. Louie's got a horse running tonight, sure thing."

Now the dress clothes he was wearing made sense. "Yeah? Sure thing, huh? Just like last time? That donkey came in last."

"This is the real deal, bro, and it won't be the last."

"You sure? I don't feel like blowing a yard on another frigging whisper."

"Unc's been working with Yuri, the Russian. He's set up a system."

"Oh, you mean like your craps system, the blackjack, system, the roulette system…"

"Don't be a wiseass. It's a lock: a fucking lock!"

Lock, another keyword that seriously underperformed. "You sure?"

"You don't wanna bet, no skin off my back."

We sailed over the Verrazano Bridge and took the Belt Parkway to Aqueduct Racetrack where he made a beeline to the handicapped parking area.

"Let me out before you park."

"What's the big deal?"

"It's not right, man. No reason to take a spot someone really needs."

He pulled into a blue space anyway and flipped a handicap card onto the dash. "Let's roll!"

I looked both ways, opened the door. "I guess mental handicap qualifies."

He bought the tickets for the box seat area, which was where you headed if anyone you knew was going to the track, otherwise it was the grandstand, saving money to throw on the ponies.

The track was only half full but had a palpable buzz and clashing smells of cigars, cigarettes and cheap food.

The seedy grandstand was full of smoke and desperation with men huddled in small groups, pawing over the racing form, animating their picks. We navigated the ticket and butt-strewn floor to the premium seats.

"There's Duke." Tommy pointed to a sharp-dressed, mountain of a man in a row on the rails. He was the only one in Louie's posse that didn't smoke. We went down front.

"Dukester, where's everybody?"

"Melon and the Worm took Lou to the doctor."

"Doctor? What for?"

"He wasn't feeling good. He spit up some blood this morning, and as soon as we got here he wasn't feeling right."

"He gonna be all right?"

"I'm sure no big deal, but your aunt was nuts this morning, so we had to be sure."

Tommy nodded. "Okay. What's the deal here?"

Duke leaned in, overwhelming us with cologne, whispering, "Fancy Dancer in the sixth."

"Yeah?"

He nodded. "I need you to lay some down." He pulled out two rubber-banded wads of cash. "Take these; there's two K each, and don't go to the same window. Don't be first in line either, you hear?"

"No sweat. We got it covered."

The loudspeaker crackled with the neck-and-neck finish of the third race as Tommy studied the program.

"You not going to bet now, are you?"

He crushed out a cigarette with his shoe. "Got to keep it interesting."

We went up to the window and he put a hundred on Wonderama while I laid down a ten for show on the longest shot in the race, Placate Me. Tommy's horse finished out of the money but my long shot came in second.

"Nice way to kick off the night! Maybe instead of reading the form you should ask me!"

"Yeah, right, you bet like a fucking accountant, you'll never make a real score."

"Hey, the idea is to go home with more than I came with!" I exchanged my ticket for seventy-four dollars.

Emboldened a bit, I hoped the night would be one to brag about and laid twenty bucks on Lucky Stars, a four to one shot for place while Tommy bet another hundred on the favorite, Beanstalk.

The script played out perfectly with Beanstalk winning by ten lengths over Lucky Stars. Tommy got back the hundred he lost and another eighty and I doubled my money, setting us up for the main event.

The board had Fancy Dancer odds at eight to one and I was making calculations,

"How much you putting down?"

"All I got, about eight hundred."

"You that sure?"

"It's a lock, man. I'm telling you."

I had about two fifty total and was ready to put it all on the line but my dad's strategy of taking some money off the table when you were ahead, gnawed at me, "Let's get the bets down for Duke first."

We split up and I got in a short line, working off the rubber band as I made it to the window. I leaned in, plopping the money on the counter, "Two thousand to win on the two horse; Fancy Dancer."

The teller punched the order in and a stream of tickets shot out. I checked the board as I shoved Duke's tickets deep in my pocket. The odds had dropped a bit, to seven to one, still a nice payoff if it held.

I went to another set of windows and placed a bet for two hundred to win and a twenty to place, ensuring I would walk away with something if the 'sure' thing happened to come in second.

We watched the tote board flash updated odds as the horses warmed up. Fancy Dancer had dropped to six to one.

"Stay there, just stay there."

The horses were led into the gate as the board flashed Fancy Dancer at five to one.

"Shit! Five to one! But it's a good sign the late money's always right, man."

"It's all good. Don't get greedy, Skins."

And they're off! The pack settles down, and it's Andy Boy out front, Tuscan Beast, Sue's Blues, Fancy Dancer, followed by Glendale and Day Dreamer, with Brio bringing up the rear.

"Come on Fancy, Come on!" I shouted.

Tuscan Beast making a move, neck and neck with Andy Boy. Here comes Fancy Dancer two wide. Glendale moving up. Andy Boy in the lead as they spin out of the first turn. Fancy Dancer making a move, passes Tuscan Beast. Sue's Blues and Day Dreaming fading and Brio way behind the pack.

The pack separates and it's Andy Boy, Fancy Dancer and Glendale up front with Tuscan, Sue's Blues, Day Dreaming and Brio. Around the final turn it's Andy Boy and Fancy Dancer fighting it out as Glendale fades fast.

And down the stretch they come! Fancy Dancer and Andy Boy neck and neck, Glendale a distant third, then it's Tuscan Beast, Sue's Blues and Day Dreaming. Brio's pulled up and out.

The crowd egged on their favorites and I burped up acid as the announcer called the finish,

Fancy Dancer by a neck, Andy Boy hanging in.

"Come on, come on, be there!" Tommy was rapping his leg with a rolled-up program.

And at the wire it's Fancy Dancer by half length, Andy Boy and Glendale…

"Fuckin A Man! That was close!" Tommy said as we high-fived.

My legs were weak as Duke nodded with a thin smile.

"Listen up. Be calm. Cash the tickets over two windows each, and run the dough into the boss. Got it?"

"Sure, no prob, Duke."

Heads held high we bounded into the Cue Shot. I left Vinny at the bar and went to see my uncle.

Louie was holding an unlit cigar, playing cards. He nodded in the direction of his private office, "Fellas, hang on I got to speak with my nephew."

Louie closed the door behind me, "Tommy, how'd it goes?"

"That Russia came through!" I put a bag of cash on his desk.

He looked in the bag, "Nice, you do okay?"

"Yeah, made a couple of bucks."

"Make sure you clean up your tab with Patsy."

"I was going to but wanted to get this to you first."

He eyed my skeptically, "You keep this quiet, understand?"

"Sure, of course Unci."

"No disrespect, but I don't even want your father to know, understand?" He hacked away and spit up some phlegm.

"Ah sure, how you feeling, Duke said you were sick?"

"I'm okay, no smoking they say. Look at this shit, even got me keeping the wrapper on it." He showed me his cigar. "I got to get back; we're in the middle of a big pot."

"Sure, sure." We headed to the door and before we stepped out I said, "Hey Unc, I'd be nice if you kept me dialed in if there's another lock at the track."

"I'll see you at the station in the morning kid."

I sidled up to Vinny, "Hey JoJo, get me a Stoli on ice and put the Nets game on, I've got five yards on my boys."

"Five hundred with Dr. J out?"

"They're overdue, man. The odds are with me. What time you got?"

"Just about nine thirty."

"Knicks playing the Lakers in LA. Suck down your drink, Spence. We got a half hour to get to the lounge."

We got back in the car and headed for Caesar's Lounge where Patsy ran a sizable gambling operation for Louie. It was a real cheesy place, and Vinny stood in the car as I went to see Patsy, paying down my tab of a grand and laying another thousand on the Knicks.

Chapter Eight

"Man, you missed some game, bro."

Tommy shrugged, keeping silent.

"The place went bazonkas when Nettles hit the slam to win it. It was really something, man."

He pulled out a cigarette and tapped it on his hand, murmuring, "So I heard."

"The stadium was shaking like a leaf; I thought it might collapse, man!"

He mumbled something unintelligible.

I didn't have the heart to torture him anymore. "Joey and Red said they're going to the San Gennaro Feast, Wednesday. You wanna go?"

"Nah, too crowded."

"All of a sudden you like things quiet?"

"I got something to do."

"Playing house with Donna?"

"Very funny. Gotta work."

"Work? Didn't know it was in your vocabulary."

"You're a real comedian tonight."

"So, tell me, what job you landed?"

"Just helping Billy again, making some dough."

I nodded, hoping like hell he'd open up, but he stared straight ahead. I kept quiet a moment longer before asking,

"So, what you doing?"

"Running smokes up."

Pictures of him walking with shopping bags full of long brown bags as a kid in the neighborhood flashed in my head.

"What? I, I don't mean to be nosy; you don't have to tell me."

"Nah, it's all right. You're one guy I don't worry about."

Worry? About me? It's him that's on the tracks for disaster, not me. He continued, "Sundays I take my old man's Chrysler and head south around two."

"South?"

"Yeah, North Carolina, make the pickup and time the return back to the Island for Monday morning, rush hour."

"Every week?"

"Yeah, no big deal, just run down and shoot back up."

The truth was Tommy had become part of a smuggling ring. He was born into it and never gave it a second thought. I was unsure whether to venture into advice dispensing, but as opinionated as I was I had to.

"You got to be careful, man. You get caught, and your ass will be behind bars."

"It's no big deal, man. I already got pinched."

"You mean arrested?"

He grinned. "Yeah, it's a fuckin' joke. All's they do is take the stash and fine you."

"Don't it go on your record?"

He shrugged. "The bitch is we lose the cargo and that hurts, and those bastards know it."

Well, I guess losing money was the one thing that wasn't a big deal. "How much is a load?"

"Forty grand."

"Get out! How the hell?"

We stopped at a light and he kept quiet. Maybe I'd pushed the questions too much. When the light turned, he gunned it saying, "We get two thousand cartons in the Chrysler.'

"Two thousand? No way."

"Yeah, we yank out the back seat, Town Cars hold even more."

"You shitting me?"

"Nah, I wanted to use a van, but Billy said no way. They're a target, stand out too much."

My mind was spinning to verify the math, it just seemed nuts. I didn't smoke but knew a pack was about six bucks, ten packs to a carton. So, sixty a carton, maybe they get a discount. With two thousand in a car that made about a hundred twenty thousand dollars. Was that right? He said forty grand.

"Skins, you know me. I'm doing the math, and it don't add up."

"What don't add up, Einstein?"

I explained my calculations, and he smirked.

"You spending too much time in the office, Otis. What you think we wet our beaks on? Forty is what we pay for the smokes."

The margin was easy to see but difficult to comprehend. A carload of cigarettes could yield a profit of over eighty thousand dollars?

"Holy shit, that leaves you with eighty grand!"

"Easy, Otis, we have expenses too." He pulled up in front of Aliotta Pastry Shop and jumped out.

I hoped he'd come back ready to talk. Five minutes later he put a stack of his mother's favorite pastries in the back seat and handed me an S cookie.

"Thanks, bro. You still into talking?"

"I ain't got to tell you to keep it quiet, okay?"

He went on to explain the numbers in a bit more detail. The whole game was basically arbitrage; they made money on the difference in tax rates, between New York whose tax per pack was well over four dollars and North Carolina where it was under fifty cents. They gave the driver, who paid the gas and tolls, a buck a carton for the run, and they had a distribution network, where they'd wholesale the cartons for ten bucks over cost.

That night I rolled around in bed trying to make sense of the money and scope of Louie's operations. I had to hand it to Louie and his gang; they knew how to rake in serious cash. It seemed easy, and as I wondered how many guys there were making runs, I found myself rationalizing away the criminal aspect. It was hard to believe that one guy making a weekly run could put a million dollars less expenses into the gang's hands.

It was clear with that much money sloshing around it spawned other opportunities like loan-sharking, which led to the takeovers of businesses whose owners couldn't repay the debt. It also provided plenty of money for bribes to buy the outcomes you wanted. There was a nasty side but I discounted it, vowing to increase my wagers when the next horse racing opportunity came along.

Chapter Nine

Yuri usually drank his morning coffee at home, but after a late night of poker in a Manhattan club he was running late. He showered, ran a razor carefully over his head and then jumped into his car to go to 7-Eleven. He poured a large cup and got online to pay. After five of the six people in line bought cigarettes with their coffee, he spawned an idea. Yuri paid for his java and got back in his Cadillac.

He sped down Victory Boulevard and pulled into a Quick Mart that a friend owned.

"Where's Boris?"

"In the back."

Yuri sipped his coffee, banged on the door and swung it open.

"Yuri! What's up, my friend?"

He nodded, thrusting his chin forward. "How you?"

"Good, good. What brings you around?"

"How's biz?"

"Pretty good here, but Eltingville is on fire."

"You're lucky son of bitch."

"Don't know about the luck, Yuri. That guy ran it down. I busted my ass turning it around, not to mention the money we spent fixing it up. You know we're buying two more; I'll fix 'em too."

"Good, listen. I got idea to get money back, increase margins."

Wary, Boris kept quiet.

"How many carton smokes you sell in month?"

"Uh, I'm not sure."

"Stop fuck with me, zhopa! You know every bag of chips you move!"

"I don't know exactly, uh say about a thousand, between both stores."

"I got connection; you save ten bucks a carton. That's load of dough."

"What?"

"Instead to make your order with the companies, you make with us."

"You getting them from the tobacco companies, a distributor?"

"Why the fuck does it matter where Yuri get."

"I, I don't know. Is this legit?"

"Don't worry. Why to pay more when you get for less? Nice, make more eight grand a month, huh?" He smiled.

"I don't know, Yuri. I gotta talk with my brother, the family."

"What the fuck? They no like money? You send more back to Moscow, you be fucking hero."

"I, I need a day. Please Yuri, let me talk with them."

A day later, Ivan paid a visit to Boris and reported in to Yuri who was eating his lunch.

"Boss, the fecking Boris said his family didn't want to get involved."

Yuri picked up a piece of smoked fish and shook his head as he chewed.

"He was really scared, Yuri. I can send some boys over to help convince him."

"Nyet, get Stephan."

Chapter Ten

Jack Lugman covered the boxing beat for the *Daily News*. Cigar usually clenched between teeth, Jack was a boxing historian whose real love was the ponies. An avid rider before a hip replacement, he'd roam the paddock area hours before the first race. Then, outfitted in a crumpled sports jacket, he'd head for the grandstand and pour over the racing forms with his track buddies. Though a daily fixture at Aqueduct, he never put more than ten bucks on a race.

Jack was at the track when a long shot came in when the front runners seemed to give up. Ten days later, when it happened again, his radar screamed. Lugman checked into it, finding the same owners were involved in both races. Though the jockeys and competing owners were not the same, his gut told him something was amiss.

The owners of the horses in question were part of a growing group of what he called hobby owners.

Race horse ownership had evolved, from serious horse breeders to wealthy hobbyists and wise guys. Lugman had a hunch these owners were squarely in the pinky-ring crowd.

While covering the early rounds of the Golden Gloves Jack made time to check into the owners' records and wasn't surprised to find they'd never had winners before the last few months. He followed the owners' horses over the next month and was convinced it wasn't the trainers who got them into the winner's circle.

Lugman had great contacts at the track and took the escalators to the top level of the racetrack. He snuffed out his cigar and entered the offices of New York's Assistant Racing Commissioner Frank Blair. The back wall of the office was all glass and provided a bird's-eye view of the track.

"How's it going?" Jack shook his friend's hand and went straight to the window. He loved the grime of the grandstand, but this view took his breath away every time he visited his friend.

"Great. Hey, that kid Hector Pancho's got some left hook."

"You saw it?"

"Nah, no need to, just read your column!" He chuckled.

"The kid can go places, but he's got to work on his footwork."

"Don't have a clue. So what else is going on?"

"Frankie, something's been bothering me, and you outta know about it."

Frankie waved him away from the window and put his feet on the desk. "Sit down."

He settled in a chair. "You know I'm here a lot."

"More than me; you should get a paycheck." He laughed.

"So, listen, I thinking maybe there some monkey business going on here. I don't know; some races just seem staged."

The assistant commissioner bolted upright, "What? Did you say fixing races?"

"I'm no alarmist; you know that, but it's worth it to take a closer look."

Jack explained his circumstantial evidence and Frankie responded, "That's all you got? A couple of owners whose horses are running well? Maybe they're just hitting their stride."

"Seven ponies at the same time?"

"The stewards didn't see anything? We've got no reports, nothing. You know, Jack, the game's a lot cleaner these days."

"All I'm asking is to watch the tapes with me. See what I'm seeing, and check the provenance of these." He pulled a piece of paper out of his shirt pocket.

"What's the angle?"

"I couldn't find any history on these. My hunch is they picked them up cheap at claiming races down south, changed names, and bingo."

Frankie assured his friend he'd check into how the owners obtained the horses in question and set a date to view the videos with Jack a week later. He walked him to the door and lowered his voice.

"Jack, I think you're maybe reading too much into this, but I'll check it out. You got to keep this under your shirt. If something's going on we can't tip anybody off."

He showed Jack out, went down the hall to the library and pulled up one of the races Jack mentioned. Frankie played the VHS and fast-forwarded to the sixth race. The race looked normal enough: three horses led most of the way, but down the stretch they lost steam, and a horse named Biscotti won by a length. Lugman was a racing student, but even the best of fans always believed the game was fixed he thought and headed back to his office.

A nephew of Boris's who ran the rush-hour shift at the second store, called Boris.

"Uncle Boris, you having the place remodeled?"

"What? Remodeled? What are you talking about?"

"There are two big trucks parked right in front of the store. There's four, five guys who cordoned off the sidewalk and put closed signs out."

"Must be mistake; talk with them."

"I did; they said you contracted with them."

"That's nonsense. You tell them…" Boris stared out the front window as a pair of trucks swung in front, blocking the sidewalk to his store. "Uh, I'll call you back."

Boris made a beeline for the gym and begged to see Yuri.

"Ah, Boris, how you, my friend?"

"I've been thinking, you know, talking about your idea."

Yuri nodded and steepled his fingers.

"Do they have stamps on 'em?" Boris knew if the packs didn't have tax stamps on them he'd run into trouble immediately.

"Who the fuck you deal with here?" Yuri rose with an evil smile as he came around his desk. "We got under control." He sat in a chair next to Boris.

"Okay, okay. I just got to be sure."

"Now, you ready to make serious dough?"

"Yeah, but If you can understand I can't just stop ordering cold turkey. If that's okay with you I mean."

Yuri worked out a deal to start supplying a couple of hundred cartons a month to Boris and by the second month Boris bought nearly 80 percent of what he was selling. By the third month he had dropped prices to the lowest in the area and was selling two thousand cartons a month.

Pleased to be able to move a large quantity of smokes without a middleman, Yuri embarked on a sort of sales campaign. He would send his toughies to convince other convenience and drugstores to buy most of the cigarettes they sold from him. It took some time and muscle, but the combo of intimidation and greed proved to be a powerful persuader, and the business and cash it generated multiplied.

Chapter Eleven

I cracked the front windows. "Wait in the car, girl. Daddy will be right back. Good girl."

After I hopped out, Grease climbed on the armrest, eyes following as I disappeared behind a door.

"Tommy boy, how's it going?"

"Good, Donnie! How's it hanging?" Donnie was the guy who ran The Flatted Fifth, a social club my dad frequented to drink and play cards. Actually, I was beat and pissed, having gotten stuck in a forty-mile backup in Virginia on the way back. My back was killing me, and I had a nasty cyst on my ass.

"Same old shit, kid."

"Billy here?"

"In the back."

"Lemme have a shot of Johnnie Black with a chaser."

I knocked down a second combo and gingerly got off my stool. "See you later, Donnie."

I called out some hellos as I walked to the rear door, knocked twice and threw it open. There was my father, playing cards with some woman hanging all over him.

"Hey, Tommy. Come on in. Joey, deal him in."

"Nah, gotta run, just stopped by to see you for a minute."

"Sit down. Hey, this is Juanita. Juanita this is my boy Thomas."

"Hiya doing?"

She giggled. "He's a cutie, Billy."

"Can we talk?" I said backpedaling a step.

"After this hand."

"Hope you got something good."

"It'd be the first one of the day."

After the next cards were dealt he folded his hand and got up.

"You okay? You got bags under your eyes."

"Just tired, long drive back. Listen. Tess, uh, Mom is pissed. You ain't been home for a week she said."

"What she bitchin' about? The bills are paid."

"Yeah? I had to give her three hundred for groceries and shit." He didn't respond, and it teed me off that he made no attempt at repayment. "It ain't right; you gotta show your face."

He took a step forward saying, "Watch your mouth! This got nothing to do with you."

"Yeah, well, you're putting me in the middle." I balled up my fists.

"You worry about you, ya hear me? Don't stick your nose in my business. Now get the hell out of here!"

I was pissed and couldn't muster the will to fake it as I stormed out. Who the hell does he think he is? He wants respect as a father? What a load of shit. He wasn't no role model for me: the crap he got me involved in. Shit, he even sucked at that.

As I approached the car, Grease pawed at the window and jumped in my lap before I was completely seated. My anger melted away after a couple of licks. *Who said you can't buy love?* Grease whimpered signaling she had to go and I grinned.

Sure enough, after just sniffing at two sets of tires she did her business. *Wait till I tell Donna.* I never thought I'd get attached to another dog and had Donna to thank for it. I remember how shitty I felt when Jackpot deteriorated and had to be put down. I fingered the impression of Jackpot's paw print in my pocket and replayed getting Grease as we drove off.

I was holding Jackpot, crying like a baby when Donna came into the room to put her down. She said it'd be a good idea to have a memory of her and suggested an impression of her paw. Not one for mementos or sentimental reflection, I said no, but she was so caring and convincing, not to mention hot looking, that I agreed.

The first days without Jackpot, after having her for sixteen years, were tough until the call from Donna.

"Tommy, it's Donna from Hylan Vet."

I felt a stir in my loins at hearing her voice. "Hey, how you doing?"

"I wanted to let you know the paw keepsake is in. I snuck a peek; it came out real nice."

"Good."

"I could mail it out…"

"Nah, I'll be down this afternoon. You'll be there, right?"

The place was crowded, and Donna was working the desk with another woman. She gave me a big smile.

"Hi, Tommy. Hang on, I'll get it." She disappeared into a room and came out holding a small velvet box.

"Here you go." She opened the box. "Looks good, huh?"

I drew back a bit, staring silently at the impression of Jackpot's small paw set in an uneven circle of yellowish ceramic. She moved closer to me and handed me the trinket.

"Whaddya think? It's nice, right?"

"I guess so; kind of weird though." I traced the print with my thumb, distracted by her sweet smell.

"I know what you mean. I remember losing my first dog. It's tough." She patted my shoulder.

"Tell me about it. It sucks."

"You know you should get another one fast."

"Nah, don't think I ever will. Don't want to get attached again."

"That's silly."

I eyed her with half a frown.

She glanced at her coworker "Mary, I'm going to the pens. Cover for me."

She yanked her thumb at me. "This way, mister."

My eyes were glued to her ass as we walked down a hallway to a small room with cages of puppies.

I stopped at the door. "No thanks, man. I ain't interested."

"Let me show you something. I think you'll love her." She took my hand and pulled me to a corner cage. I was thinking of making a move on her as she said, "These two are Italian greyhound, they're really special. A customer's dog just had a litter. They need a home, and she is only looking for a hundred. Normally, these are five hundred or more depending on the breeding."

"They get big though."

"Not these guys; they're miniatures, only get to five, six pounds, max." She bent down, and her skirt crept up, exposing creamy skin. She opened the door and reached in, hiking her skirt and my desire higher, and came out with a handful of puppy.

"Not that one, get the other one," I said, pointing to the one with sad-looking eyes.

Donna passed the camel-colored ball of life to me. She was light as a feather, and her belly was red hot. She was barely bigger than my hand but had a long tail shaped in a U.

"What's her name?"

"Don't have one yet."

She licked my wrist nonstop. "We'll call her Grease."

She frowned. "Grease? I don't know…"

"It's a betting term, means a bribe. This little girl's gonna be a bribe to me to get over Jackpot."

She giggled. "Whatever it takes."

"Hey, what d'you say we grab a drink when you're done? Celebrate my new puppy?"

Chapter Twelve

Lewis Goldbaum, the district attorney for New York City, applied a coating of lip balm as the jury filed silently back into the courtroom and took their seats. Judge Fortunato queried the foreman,

"Have you reached a verdict?"

He offered a document. "Yes, Your Honor."

Goldbaum resisted the urge to straighten his new tie. He forced his shoulders back and held his breath as the bailiff handed off the decision to the judge.

The judge glanced at the document, looked up and read it out loud.

"On the count of conspiring to commit fraud—guilty. Two counts of bribery—guilty. Obstruction of justice—guilty…"

Goldbaum let out a sigh of relief before being glad-handed by his assistant DA.

"Nice going, Lew!"

"You nailed the dirty SOB!"

"Thanks. This is a win for the good citizens of New York." Goldbaum kept a serious face on as he spit out the first of many practiced sound bites and looked forward to getting in front of the cameras on the courthouse steps.

The DA was on a roll. He'd handpicked a couple of high-profile cases to try himself, knowing they would elevate his stature in the city. Each case carried the risk of tarnishing his reputation but Goldbaum chose them carefully, calibrating the downside and throwing the considerable resources of his office behind them. The current mayor was in his second term, and speculation on who the next mayor would be was building.

Putting Brock, who had bilked the city out of two hundred million dollars, behind bars would cement him into the top tier of likely candidates.

The state and city needed the win. Their budgetary woes were national news, and the city itself was losing its prominence. New York had lost a lot of people and business to the Sunbelt over the last decade, and the toll wreaked havoc on its finances. The Brock verdict would hopefully begin the turn of the tide.

As Goldbaum ate his breakfast he smiled. He could not have crafted a better headline that the one the *Daily News* used; 'Golden Boy Bags Bloodsucker Brock,' for its morning paper. He went to get dressed for the stream of interviews he'd do, already thinking past the mayor's office to the governorship.

Tommy bounded through Cue Shot's front door. It was eerily quiet, even though it was two deep at the bar.

"Hey, what's this, a funeral?"

Heads turned with looks of disapproval as Sammy the Snake urgently waved me over.

"Where's the casket, bro?"

"God forbid!" He hung his head. "You don't know, huh?"

"What? What the hell going on?"

'It's Louie; he's sick, really fucking sick."

"What's wrong?"

"Cancer, man, in the frigging throat."

I sucked deeply on my cigarette, stared at it and ground it out. "He gonna be all right?"

"We hope so, got the best fucking doctors in the city. Dr. Mikey hooked him up…"

I blocked out the rest and threw up a hand as a goodbye.

"Tommy! Louie will be so happy to see you." Her eyes were red, and she didn't have a stitch of makeup on.

"Hey, Aunt Jo, don't worry. He'll be all right. He's tough as they come."

"I know, I know, but I donno. I'm just scared, I guess. The history's not good. It's like we're cursed."

"You got to be strong, man. It's the only way. Where is he?"

She hiked a thumb. "The den."

The den was as dark as the mood in the house. Louie was in a recliner, covered by a blanket staring at a muted TV. There was a mug of something surrounded by balls of tissues. Startled, he bolted upright, clearing his throat.

"Tommy, good to see you. How's your mother and father?"

"They're okay."

"You sure? I'm hearing things."

"Yeah, sure. You know Billy."

He wagged his head. "He's a piece of work."

I sat down. "How you doing, Unc?"

"The doc says it's bad, but I can beat it. I donno…"

"Shit, yeah. You'll beat it! You're like steel!"

"Yeah, we'll see. The family's got a bad record with this shit."

"The odds are with you, then. It all evens out, you know. You're on a losing streak, then you get hot…"

He shifted in his chair and spit into a tissue. "I hope you're right. But since you brought it up, there's something that's been bothering me."

"Sure, what's up?"

"Listen, kid. You know I love you, but you got to put an end to this fucking gambling. You just can't be trusted if you're always in the hole. It doesn't look good. You understand?"

"It's not that bad, I…"

He swept his finger under his throat. "Stop the bullshit." He leaned toward me. "I'm gonna tell Moose to wipe the slate clean, you hear? But just this one time. That's it, the end, finito. No more bets for you. The guys won't take your bets."

I owed over eight thousand and was grateful but felt a stab at being cut off. "Oh okay, thanks."

"Don't breathe a word of this to nobody, especially to your father. You know I tried with him, but he never frigging learns." He shook his head as his voice trailed off, and I changed the subject.

Just a week later I took Tess, who'd cooked up a storm of soft foods, to see Louie. Smelling the escarole and beans as we climbed the stairs opened my appetite, and I hoped my aunt would dish some out. But when we saw him laid out on a couch, I lost my hunger. It could've been my mind playing tricks, but he looked like hell, a lot worse in only a week.

Louie propped himself up and when my aunt adjusted the pillows. I shot a glance at Tess who was tearing up. I quickly shook my head at her to stop the nonsense and pulled up a chair.

"Hey, Unc, my mom cooked up some nice dishes for you. You hungry?"

"I made him some soup when we came back from the doctor's."

"What the doc say?"

"Tuesday, we got an appointment to get some steroid injections, to help with his strength and stuff, and then Thursday he's getting this new chemo, and they think it's gonna work…"

I looked at my uncle who, chin on chest, had fallen asleep as my aunt droned on. I got up to go to the bathroom when the doorbell rang.

"Tommy, can you get it? Should be Yuri."

Sure enough, the Russian had come to visit. We bullshitted a bit, but he only stayed a few minutes before handing off an envelope of cash, in full view of my aunt, on the way out.

Mayor Price was appreciative for the respite in bad news and invited the DA to his weekly press conference. He hoped having Goldbaum there would shift the attention away from New York's budgetary woes.

It didn't work as the mayor was taking a beating with his plan to shut down a dozen fire houses and cut the police force.

"My administration has studied the impact of any closures. We're confident that if—and I repeat, if—we have to combine any districts, the impact will be minimal. Please, rest assured that we are working nonstop to find ways to maintain services at their current levels. I have asked every department to scrutinize their budgets for savings and efficiencies. Look at the wonderfully important work our district attorney's office has been doing." Anxious to get out of the spotlight he said, "Lewis, come up to the podium. I'm sure there are a few questions for you."

Goldbaum pulled in his smile a bit as he strode to the podium fingering the tube of ChapStick in his pocket.

"Thank you, Mr. Mayor. I would like to confirm what His Honor stated; the orders are clear about reducing waste across all departments of government. Trust me; they are putting the heat on all of us to deliver!" Goldbaum gestured as if wiping his brow.

The room erupted in laughter, and when it petered out, a reporter from WPIX asked, "Mr. Goldbaum, do you really think it's possible to balance the books without raising taxes or reducing services?"

"If we can root out fraud and corruption, we can maintain the current level of services. That means no cuts, period." He sneaked a peek at Gordon Black, his chief of staff, who gave a thumbs-up.

"Are you implying that fraud and corruption are rampant?"

"No, but we do have efforts underway to identify areas of concern."

"Can you share anything with us?"

Goldbaum had stretched the truth and ran for cover. "Gentlemen, you know I'm unable to comment on ongoing investigations."

The news over the following weeks was filled with speculation about another big case coming out of the DA's office. It was the fairy-tale ending everyone hoped for; some unknown hole would be magically plugged, sparing New York citizens from tax hikes or cuts in service. The media promptly dispatched legions of reporters to scour the city for leads on what they hoped would be the story of the year.

Chapter Thirteen

"Hey, Nance, it's Tommy. He wants to know if we want Chinese or pizza."

"He's coming over again?" She made a face.

"What do you want to eat?"

"Not hungry."

"Get some pizza, hon, but don't get too much, and no pepperoni. Yeah, okay. See you later."

"What's the matter, Nance?"

"He's been here like every night for the last month, and that dog."

"So, what's the problem?"

"Aw, come on, Donna! You can do better than him!"

"Tommy's good. He cares about me. You don't understand him."

"Yes, I do! He's a gambler and a drunk."

"That's bullshit!"

"Bullshit? He gets whacked every night, and you join in most of the time."

"What are you talking about, joining in? Like I'm some sort of degenerate?"

"Listen, Don, you're my sister. I love you, but he's a bad influence on you. I just want things good for you."

"Yeah, don't worry about me," Donna said as she got out paper plates and napkins.

Nance headed for the door. "Well, I do."

"Where you going?"

"Out."

"But the food's coming." The door slammed shut.

The door opened, and Grease scampered into the apartment.

"Yo, babe."

"Hey, Grease. Come here, girl." She scooped up the greyhound. "Tommy, you got too much food; I said not to get too much."

"Yeah, I know, couldn't resist the calzones!"

Tommy put the boxes down and changed the channel to the Mets game. "Where's Nance?"

"Uh, she went out."

When he saw the score he said, "These fucking mutts lost three in a row; now they got to play like all-stars when I'm on the other side?"

He went to the refrigerator. "You want a brew?"

"Nah. Did you hear about the new pope? He's from Poland."

"Great, a damn Pollack." He popped the beer and took a long guzzle. "Time to chow. I'm starved."

After Tommy downed four beers with his food, he had Donna do his nails before they retreated to the sofa and TV.

Nancy came back to the apartment just after nine, finding Tommy and Donna on the couch, nestled under a blanket. Grease shook the sleep out as Tommy called out, "Yo, Saint Nancy. How's it going?"

She headed to the bedroom without speaking.

"What's up her ass?"

"She thinks you're here too much."

"Yeah, well fuck her."

"Oh, come on, Tommy. She's my sis, and she's worried about me."

"Well, she'll be happy I'm going." He got up and put his pants on as Grease hopped off the couch.

"Going? Where you going?"

"Card game at Stubs. Come on, girl." The door slammed shut again.

Behind his Aqueduct desk, Frank Blair was on the phone when he flipped over his calendar. *Shit! Jack will be here at five.*

He finished up the call and hustled over to the library. Rummaging through the drawers he pulled out four cartridges of microfiche and popped one into a microfilm reader. He paged through the documents on it and magnified the background of Moscow's Queen. It showed the mare was born in Kentucky and originally named Winston. She raced around the third-string racing circuit, never placing higher than fifth when she was claimed by someone named Igor Desenavich for five thousand dollars. He jotted a note but wasn't alarmed until he viewed two others. He made further notes, returned the cartridges and went to the video section.

"Hey, Frankomino. How you doing?"

"Menza a menza. Put that cigar out and close the door."

Jack stubbed the cigar out, closed the door and headed to the wall of windows. "Looks like it might rain."

"Come on, let's watch some TV." He pointed to the stack of video tapes. "Any particular order?"

"Nah, what'd you get on the provenance?"

Frankie popped a tape in. "Pretty much a bunch of hags struggling to compete in the minors."

"Really? Any patterns on the sellers? The tracks? Anything like that?"

He raised a hand. "Easy. It doesn't prove a thing. What happens on the turf is what counts."

"Shit! I forgot to tell you to check the urine samples."

"Hey, who you dealing with? Checked the reports, all clean," Frankie said as he fast-forwarded to the race in question.

The horses exploded out of the gates, and both men inched closer to the screen. The race unfolded, and the pack came out of the first turn.

"I think it's coming up, slow it down."

Frankie put it on slow motion. "Nothing I see."

"There. See right there." Jack pointed. "Go back. Back up!"

"Shush, take it easy." Frankie hit the rewind button.

"See the leaders are all dropping back at the same time."

"I donno. You're reading too much into it."

"No way, man. I've seen thousands of races; you too. It just doesn't happen like that. Pop another in; you'll see."

They watched five races, and though a pattern seemed obvious to Jack, his friend remained concerned but unconvinced.

Chapter Fourteen

It wasn't the white knight the city was looking for, and it wasn't a reporter who unearthed a disturbing trend. Instead, it was a tax accountant striding through the canyons of lower Manhattan with a sheaf of papers.

Sixtyish Giacomo Birelli was a serious man who sported a white goatee and had worked downtown in New York's excise tax and revenue division for over thirty years. Though never promoted to higher office, he maintained a zeal for bean counting.

He arrived precisely at 10 a.m. at the district attorney's third-floor office in city hall and noted the DA's upscale furnishings as he was shown to Assistant DA Ronald Turbow's office.

"Hello, Jack. Grab a chair. Susie, can you get us a couple of coffees?"

"Hello, Mr. Turbow. Make mine black, please. By the way, the name's Giacomo."

"Err, sorry, Giacomo."

"No problem. Most make the same assumption."

Turbow settled in his chair. "You mentioned it was important, so what d'you have?"

"Well, you see, Mr. Turbow. I've been handling the excise taxes for the last decade, and though the total amount we collect has risen slightly, I drilled down a bit."

"Uh-huh, go on."

"Well, it's not surprising the collection of cigarette taxes, which include cigars and loose tobacco, have come down. On the surface people are smoking a bit less, but when you factor in the dramatic rise in the rate of tax per pack, it doesn't add up. You know we raised it by over three dollars a pack and should be collecting significantly more."

Giacomo unfolded a large spreadsheet. "I've highlighted the quarterly receipts and the corresponding tax rates. Then I've normalized the tax rate factoring the decline in smoking. I've used the national numbers for that and…"

"Hold up, Giacomo. You're losing me. I'm not a numbers guy, and I appreciate the work you've obviously put into this. But in layman's terms, can you tell what you found?"

The accountant stroked his goatee. "Well, to summarize it, and I have the data to back it up; tobacco tax money's going uncollected."

Turbow wanted a summary, but this was a bit thin. "Can you give me a little more than that?"

"We know that cigarette consumption is down, so let's estimate it at five percent over the last couple of years, okay?"

"Sure, that seems fair."

"Good, so all things equal, in other words the tax rate per pack didn't change. We should realize a collection rate of five percent lower. Understand?"

"Of course."

"Well, the problem or issue is that we have tripled the tax rate and are still collecting below norm."

The coffee came in as Turbow asked, "How much we talking about here?"

Giacomo took a sip. "It a tough number to nail down exactly."

"An estimate—give me an estimate."

Giacomo tilted his head and thumbed his goatee. "Well, anywhere from two to four hundred million."

Turbow leaned forward. "Are you shitting me? That'll plug the city's budget hole…"

Giacomo put his hand up. "Hold your horses, Mr. Turbow. The estimate includes both state and city losses…"

"What's the breakdown?"

"The state tax rate is approximately seventy-five percent, so figure a hundred fifty to three hundred million for the state and fifty to a hundred million in losses for the city."

"This could be big. How certain do you feel about the likelihood these losses are real?"

"Mr. Turbow, I take my responsibilities seriously. I don't make assertions without the facts to support them."

"I, I didn't mean to imply otherwise, but this could be a hot issue, and we've got to be certain before we begin throwing manpower at it."

"Rest assured, I have tripled checked the statistics and even verified collection rates for other states: states that have raised rates as we have, with similar demographics, like California and Illinois."

"Wow, this is good. Really good. Listen, I've got a meeting in ten with the DA, but you can be sure I will be in touch."

"Morning, Ron."

"Morning, boss. Listen, something's come up, and it could be big. Mind if I jump right into it?"

As Turbow told Goldman about his meeting with Giacomo, the district attorney calculated the impact on New York's fiscal situation and his career aspirations. He salivated at the chance to shine in a situation that affected both the state and city. It was a rare opportunity, but he reminded himself to be cautious.

He steepled his fingers. "Uhm, it's both disturbing and hopeful."

Turbow was at the edge of his seat. "It could be huge, boss. Let's pounce on it; we could take some investigators off the board of ed case."

Goldbaum wanted to pursue it will all his guns but said, "We need to go slow here. Ask Marty to meet with this fellow Giacomo and vet the data. Then we'll go from there. Now, the Gluken hearing is coming up, and I'd like you to head it up. It's a big case, and it'll help advance your career."

After his meeting with Turbow, the DA asked his secretary to clear his schedule till noon and he worked the phones. He called a former district attorney of Arizona who had experience in the battle to prevent the Indian reservations in Nevada from running tax-free smokes into Arizona. Goldbaum also reached out to his contacts in the Florida capitol of Tallahassee. Florida had a smallish tax on cigarettes but a long border with Georgia, who had the lowest tax on tobacco in the country. The difference of ten dollars a carton provided many smugglers with an income. The DA then had a discussion with an old classmate who now headed the federal government's Alcohol, Tobacco, Firearms and Explosives interdiction efforts.

The morning was evaporating, and he made two last calls, one that canceled a lunch date with his wife, replacing her with a trusted associate for a sandwich in his office. He then met with his chief of staff, Gordon Black, who also headed the DA's exploratory committee for mayor. When Black heard the news about the tobacco tax he knew it could vault both of them into the mayor's office and pushed Goldbaum to drop other investigations and pursue it immediately. Well aware of the political implications, the DA advised he was quietly going to collect some intelligence first and left for his informal lunch date.

"Hi, come on in. How you doing, Raymond?"

"Good, Chief. Hey, thanks for inviting me up to such hallowed ground!" He shook the DA's hand.

"Let's sit over there; Sandy's organized a nice little lunch for us."

Raymond Perrilli, a veteran of two wars and countless skirmishes with organized crime, sported a crew cut and was in Navy Seal shape.

"Nice going putting that bastard Brock on ice. How long you think he's gonna get?"

"Well, the sentencing hearing is a couple of weeks away, and the defense is working overtime for leniency. But the magnitude of the fraud virtually mandates twenty years, and I think the judge is going to be sympathetic to our case."

"He should rot in the can."

"Help yourself to a sandwich, Raymond."

"So, what's cooking? I know you didn't invite me in for the chow." He grabbed a handful of fries.

"You know I value your loyalty and discretion, Raymond. Something's come to our attention, but it's early, and we need to be dead certain before we use any of this office's resources, understand?"

"Since the old neighborhood days, I've been invisible. That's why they call me Casper."

Goldbaum leaned across the table. "If what I suspect is true, we'll need the element of surprise. We can't tip our hand. Otherwise we'll be left prosecuting a bunch of low-level thugs."

Ray put down his sandwich. "I get it; what's the mission?"

"I want you to nose around, discreetly, with your organized-crime contacts. Seems a lot more smuggling of cigarettes is going on than we thought. New York is being deprived of a mountain of money, and you know the shape of our finances."

"There's a lot of players in that arena: a couple of mob families, the Chinks, a few Ruskies, and now even the Indians are moving smokes," he said between bites.

"Yes, but we suspect one organization is responsible; the sources and distribution required for this level of volume support the thesis, but I'm, we're not discounting a coordinated effort or a loose affiliation of some sort."

While eating half of a sandwich, Goldbaum shared most of the background he had learned with Ray and said he had to leave for another meeting.

Ray nodded, picked up the last quarter of his turkey club and said as the DA got up. "Leave it with me. I'll fish out a trail for you; don't you worry."

Chapter Fifteen

A month later, Nancy jumped out of bed. She jammed her feet into her slippers and hustled to the bathroom where she found Donna hugging the toilet bowl.

"What's the matter?"

"I don't know. Maybe the sausage."

"You got drunk again, didn't ya?"

"Come on, Nance. You saw me. I was fine, had just one beer."

"Aw right, you feelin' any better?"

"A bit."

"Let's get you in the shower; it'll do you good."

The sickness continued through the week, and Donna finally confided in Nancy.

"Nancy, I've got to tell you something."

"What? What's going on?"

"I, I missed my period."

"Holy shit! Are you fucking kidding me?"

"Slow down, Tommy."

"What's the big deal, man? You want one?"

"I told you I didn't feel good. Shouldn't have partied so hard last night."

"Heh heh, yeah. Good thing your old-maid sis wasn't around. That blow was awesome. What'd we do, three packs?"

Donna nodded with a frown.

"Guess you can't hang with the big dogs!"

Donna checked the clock; it was only eight o'clock, and he was already into a second six-pack, "There's gotta be a limit. What's this, four nights in a row?"

"Yeah, you're right." He hung his head, put his beer down and collapsed on a recliner. "I donno. Sometimes nothing makes sense."

"What doesn't make sense?"

"I don't know; everything's just fucked up."

"What's the matter, baby?"

"Ah, nothing."

She patted the couch. "Come here; sit by me."

He got up, smiling. "What are you, a shrink now?" Tommy sat down putting his hand in her crotch. "Now this makes sense."

She took his hand from between her legs and held it, looking directly into his bloodshot eyes. "You can talk to me, Tommy. You always hold back. Everything's a frigging joke, but I know you're hiding."

"Peek-a-boo." He grabbed his beer and took a swig.

"Listen to me. Look at me. I love you and hope you feel the same way I do. Do you?"

He nodded.

"Okay, you. We gotta trust each other. You can tell me anything—no secrets."

He looked down, took another guzzle and opened up.

"Just same old bullshit with my old man."

He told her that his father had left his mother, moving in with another woman.

"He even brought the bitch to my uncle's house when he knew Tess would be there."

"Oh no! Your poor mother. She must have boiled over."

"Yeah, and you should have seen Louie. Man, was he pissed."

Tommy felt good unloading to Donna and even better when they jumped in the sack.

A baby-blue Eldorado pulled up and double-parked in front of the Cue Shot. Yuri and his sidekick Ivan, a blond-haired mass of muscle, popped out. One of Louie's guys said, "Hey, Yuri, the boss don' want nobody double-parking."

Yuri brushed past him as Ivan glanced menacingly at the comment, opening the door for his paymaster.

They marched to the room in the back where Louie usually held court. Sitting outside the door, reading the paper was an older man who had been racked by a severe stroke. Louie gave him menial jobs to do affording him to safeguard his pride. He struggled to get to his feet when he saw the Russians coming. Ivan was about to push him aside when Yuri raised a hand.

"Ah, Marco, how you?"

"Good, the boss knows you're coming?" He knocked twice, stuck his head in and swung open the door.

"Go ahead, fellas."

"Yuri, my friend. Sit on down. Frankie, pour 'em some wine; it's a nice Brunello."

"Nyet, vodka."

Louie cleared his throat. "Get the Stoli, in the freezer."

When the glasses were full, Louie raised his glass.

"To my Russian friend, or should I say comrade?" He chuckled and clinked glasses. "A great plan and execution, Yuri."

"We talk?"

"Sure." He put his still-wrapped cigar back in his mouth.

"In private."

'Yuri, you know everybody here."

"We talk alone. Okay?"

Louie swept his hand, and Giorgio, Two-Ton Tony, and Johnny Boy got up. "Wait outside, fellas."

"Sure, boss."

Someone murmured, "You dying or something Yuri? A priest came around the station looking for you."

Ivan took a step toward the men. "Svolochs!"

"Easy, Ivan. Sit, no waste energy."

When they were alone Yuri raised his shot glass. "To Italian friend."

Louie kept his glass on the table. "What's going on, Yuri?"

"Things, they are going good. No?"

Louie raised his chin up in acknowledgment, "Pretty good."

"Pretty good? The money, it's rolling in from smokes, and my deal at track is nice. No?"

"Like I said, things are pretty good. Always can be better."

Yuri pointed to his glass, and Ivan poured another shot. Yuri dipped his finger in and put it to his lips. "You know, Louie. vodka's good for health." He threw back the drink, leaned forward and narrowed his eyes,

"I can no longer wait; I go ahead with plan we discussed."

Louie stiffened. "But we agreed not to."

"I changed mind."

"It's trouble. You'll drag…"

He patted Louie's arm. "You worry about you; Yuri worry about Yuri."

Chapter Sixteen

The cigarette business steadily grew as politicians increased the taxes put on each pack, leading to the expansion of the gang's enterprise into Queens, Brooklyn and parts of New Jersey. The cash rolled in, strengthening Yuri's position at a time that Louie's health kept him away from the operations.

I'd been in training down in Dallas for my job and hadn't seen Tommy in over three weeks. "You look like warmed-over dog shit."

"Thanks, cuz, you really know how to make a guy feel good."

"Seriously, you look beat, man. What's going on?"

He yawned widely. "Yeah, well, I made three runs this past week alone."

"Three?"

"Yeah, Knob Head. Yuri's got the smokes in a ton of convenience stores. I tell you, it's like selling fucking candy."

Yeah, I thought,. *Candy that would kill you.* "Well, at least your bank account's full."

"Ah, not really."

"What d'you mean?"

"Just a lot a shit going on, that's all."

"You've always been nigger-rich, bro. It's like holding water in your hands with you."

"What you come back from the ranch to do, hassle me?"

"It's just, you know, you have to find something that you can build around, man."

"I ain't no businessman like you, Otis."

"You don't have to be. There's a lot of things to do to make money. What are you going to be doing, driving up cigarettes when you're sixty?"

"Billy's been at it a while," he said sheepishly.

I wanted to point out how that worked out for his family but knew it wouldn't help. "You really think there's going to be any money in it in a couple of years, if it lasts that long?"

"I'll slide into something else."

"You can't go from scheme to scheme, man. One day it's going to catch up with you."

"It's what I know." His voice faded. "Maybe I should've stayed in school like you."

"There's plenty you can do; you just have to decide what kind of life you want."

"Guess so, but if I can get one nice score…"

"Stop dreaming, man! I hate to tell you, but it takes hard work."

"I ain't dreaming. I bust my ass doing this shit, and it's never enough. My mother needs help now that fucking Billy took off." He slammed a hand on the steering wheel. "Nancy left, so we're taking over the place and…"

"It's tough being an adult."

"Sucks. Change the fucking subject, all right? Did you see JR down there in Dallas?"

"We were on this campus that was incredible: everything you need, even a baseball field. It was a good trip, and I'm back down next week for a month."

"Don't come back a hick cowboy."

Tommy picked me up at JFK Airport in a new Firebird.

"Nice wheels, bro. You hit the lottery?"

He smiled broadly as he opened the trunk, "Finally on a lucky streak."

I could only fit my largest piece in the tiny trunk and had my carry-on sitting on my lap. Tommy always like to press his luck when gambling.

"What you hit, a round robin?"

"Nah, better than that. The Russian's been delivering at the track."

"Like a couple of weeks ago with Duke?"

"Yep. Maybe I found my calling."

You had to love the characterization, but I wasn't going to challenge it.

"Don't forget me on the next one."

"Sure, maybe I can get one big payday and get out of the rackets."

Five days later, Tommy's car horn blared, and I ran outside.

"Hustle, hustle! Get your money, man!"

"What's up?"

"Aqueduct! Get your money and move it!"

I ran into the house,

"Mom, how much money you got?"

"What's the matter?"

"Nothing, nothing. I just, uh, listen, Mom, I got a tip." She cocked her head and I continued, "It's a sure thing. I did it twice already." It was only once, but I needed to sell it fast: "and just want you to make some easy money."

She eyed me skeptically. "This involve Tommy? You're smarter than this…"

"Come on, Mom. You know me; I'm careful. I gotta run. If you want to do it…"

She grabbed her bag. "Here's eighty dollars, but if it's not gonna work out don't take a chance. We need it."

I flew back down the stairs, and before the door was closed he hit the gas.

"Knob Head has another pony running."

"You get it from him?"

"Nah, the commie's too much of a big shot now, putting people between him, gives him some deniability. He told my unc, and my aunt tipped me off; Yuri wants it quiet."

"This shit's a hand grenade, man; a little leak and the FBI is involved. Surprised he doesn't just keep it to himself."

"You know, this Yuri, he's cunning bastard. He's kissing Louie's ass on one hand and trying to take over his action at the same time."

"Well, sure nice to have your aunt, huh?"

"Yeah, but she's got me laying down bets for her." He laughed. "If Louie found out he'd go ballistic."

"How's he doing?"

"Not good. I'm worried when he goes, how I'm going get Yuri's information."

So much for familial love. "Not sure how long this can last anyway, bro. Anyway, who we riding tonight?"

The meal ticket was Buck Shot who was running at Aqueduct in the second race. We got there just as the gun sounded for the first race and headed to the general admission area to avoid anybody from the Island. Buck Shot opened at eight-to-one odds, and as the dirty money was laid down, it shrunk to five to one. We put down our bets, carefully splitting the action over a few tellers. I laid down almost a thousand dollars and began doubting my sanity as the horses pulled into the gate.

Buck Shot came out of the gates on top but was quickly challenged by Leprechaun on the first turn. My heart sank, and Tommy cursed as our pony faltered, veering to the center of the pack as the race wore on. As they rounded the final turn he was in third, two lengths behind, and I was in full panic mode, regretting both my mother's involvement and my large wager. I shot a glance at Tommy, who was rocking on the balls of his feet as the announcer called the finish.

Meteor and Gold Knot neck and neck. Buck Shot a length and a half back, followed by Gutsy, Hibiscus, Ranger and Sea Salt. Leprechaun pulls up. Meteor and Gold Knot slowing as Buck Shot gains.

Down the stretch it's Gold Knot by a nose over Meteor, with Buck Shot closing fast.

The crowd gasped as Meteor and Gold Knot slowed dramatically. I glanced at Tommy who was smiling as the announcer called the end of the race without comment.

Meteor and Gold Knot falter as Buck Shot bolts past to win by a half length. Then it's Grassland to place, followed by Meteor, Hibiscus, Ranger, Gutsy and Sea Salt at the rear.

"Shit, that was pretty obvious."

Before Tommy could respond, the loudspeaker system blared out.

The results have not been certified; an inquiry has been made. Hold your tickets.

A yellow light flashed on the tote board as the horses circled the track.

"What the fuck?"

"What's going on, Skins?"

"Fucking steward's inquiry!"

"In English."

"The officials who watched the race saw something, and now they want to review the fucking tape."

"You think they know?"

"Take it easy. Could be anything."

I leaned in close. "It looked too obvious, man."

"It's gonna be okay. Don't worry."

"I hope so. I got a frigging grand on the line."

The crowd's noise level and animation rose to a feverish pitch and fell off when the loudspeaker crackled.

After a review, the steward has disqualified…

An muffled sound made it impossible to tell if it was Gold Knot or Buck Shot who was disqualified.

"What he say?" both of us said simultaneously. "I don't know."

Tommy yelled to a group staring at a monitor next to us. "Hey you, what he say? Who the fuck won?"

Chapter Seventeen

Yuri went down to the gym to greet a busload of kids from the projects. He felt children really benefitted from seeing the hard work and discipline at work in his gym. Yuri had made the full day's outing a weekly event and made sure the kids had lunch and dinner before leaving with a bag full of trinkets.

After an hour with them he went to observe one of the younger boxers in his stable. Paquito Rivera was a promising heavyweight without a loss in his first five professional fights. He watched him spar for half an hour, and the kid was impressive. When he went to work on the speed bag Yuri spoke with his trainer.

"Gus, this Rivera's got the goods, no?"

"It's early, but if he puts in the work, he could break through."

"Work jab, it's sloppy."

"Yeah, it's come a long way though. We're gonna focus on that and the footwork. He gets it down, he moves right up in the ranks."

"How long will it take?"

"Ah, a couple of months…"

"Can he get ready for Quarry-Norton date? Buster Smith broke hand and pulled out, Bruno look for replacement."

"He was up against Floyd?"

"Yeah, a bum."

"Still dangerous but way past his prime. I'll have Rivera more than ready."

Yuri pulled some strings and got Rivera as a fill-in on one of the undercards for the Jerry Quarry-Ron Lyle match. It was coup, and

Yuri heavily promoted his fighter and gym, hanging banners outside the building and pushing posters into most Staten Island businesses. The Island got behind Rivera, who was born in Port Richmond, and he became a mini celebrity. Yuri enjoyed the attention the gym and his fighter received, and although he knew it was good for his image, he stayed out of the media spotlight.

The tote board flashed the order of finish and we high-fived each other.

"Shit, that was scary."

"You got no faith, man. Knob Head always comes through; it's a lock."

I nodded. My nerves were shot. I wasn't cut out for this. I knew there was no easy money, but this was easier than most ways to make it. "Let's cash in, man."

We made a beeline for the windows to collect as the monitors flashed pictures of Buck Shot heading to the winner's circle.

I didn't lay a penny down the rest of the night, keeping my hand on the wad in my pocket, but Tommy gave some back. We left the track, and he wanted to go out, but I just wanted to get home and give my mother the money she won, so I told him I had a stomach ache.

My mother was happy to get the four hundred she won and didn't press me for details. I was proud to make her some easy money. Take that back, it was nerve racking, but with my gut telling me it would end badly I only involved her once more, though I participated in five more scores.

Chapter Eighteen

Ray reported back to Goldbaum in a week, taking a seat in front of the DA's desk.

"Raymond, this is quicker than usual."

"Come on, give me some credit. My contacts are rock solid."

"Indeed. What did you learn?"

"Smokes are pouring into New York. No question, couple of gangs, as I suspected, but the Staten Island boys are moving a ton. They ramped it up significantly over the last year or so."

"Ruffino?"

He nodded. "Yeah, it's Louie Ruffino, though he's sick, cancer, seems pretty serious. They hooked up with the Russians out of Brooklyn, with Yuri Popov as the driving force in the expansion."

"How are they doing this?"

"Believe it or not, simply using mules to drive 'em up and some hijacking, though the cigarette companies have taken measures to stop having their trucks hit."

The DA applied a coating of lip balm as Pirelli offered, "These guys seem pretty disciplined. The Island's a good place to base their ops. They can run them in from Jersey, or go direct into the city. They're even running a little north, through Connecticut at times."

"Did you learn anything on their supply sources?"

"Tell you the truth, boss, didn't even check. There's no shortage of guys willing to sell down South."

"How about distribution?"

"Traditional, push most through neighborhood captains, who sell them carton by carton. Though there seems to have been a major move into direct retail, bodegas, convenience stores, mostly mom and pops. The retailers seem eager for better margins despite the risk."

Goldbaum folded his hands and tapped his thumbs. "Greed is a powerful motivator."

Ray looked at him, almost responding that power was just as enthralling. "Bingo; it's tripped up most crooks over the years. You know it's the inside secret of law enforcement. You can get away with a lot if you don't push it. Most people could get away with one or two felonies, but the schemers always push it. If they stopped at one or two we'd probably never catch—"

"This office cannot tolerate any attempts, no matter the number, to circumvent the law."

"Of course. Of course. Just saying…"

"I'd like to put together a task force. It's got to be ultraquiet though, and Lindenberry would head it. I'd like to keep you involved; your contacts and let's say, street savvy, would help to round out the picture for those on the legal side of things."

"Sure. Count me in."

"Excellent. Though it's discreet, I want this to be a priority of my office. There'll be a meeting Tuesday morning; for cover we'll use the park department's second-floor conference room."

The first meeting of the task force was controlled by the DA and his chief of staff. Although all other task forces were farmed out to deputies, Goldbaum wanted direct reporting and limited action to take place without his approval. Once that was established he asked for suggestions on strategies to stop the illegal cigarette flow. Goldbaum had his own ideas and steered the task force to a slow approach to shutting down the smuggling. The district attorney hoped to ensnare a low-level perpetrator to use as a witness against Louie Ruffino or Yuri Popov. Such a coup would disrupt their other illegal operations and provide another high-profile case for Goldbaum.

The DA finished the meeting and went to see the mayor and key members of the city council. He walked up the grand staircase envisioning a trailing entourage when he became mayor and suppressed a smile.

Goldbaum pushed through a mahogany door bearing a brass plate with the mayor's name, and a secretary ushered him to a conference room.

"Good afternoon, Mr. Mayor." He nodded toward the other two men. "Howard, Patrick."

"Sit down; we've got to get going. An officer's been wounded: nothing serious, but if I take too long to make a statement or visit, the PBA's up my bloody ass."

"I'm sorry to hear about it." Another flash forward of him at the bedside of an officer popped in his head. "This won't take long. Gentlemen. I'd like your help in drafting a small piece of legislation."

"Lew, you know the process starts in committee; what's this about?" Howard Fineman, the speaker of the city council, was already losing patience.

"Of course, but I would hope some discretion would be helpful in achieving—"

"Discretion?" The minority leader's voice was soaked in skepticism.

"Patrick, I'm not suggesting anything unethical, just some cooperation in solving the city's problems."

The mayor tapped his watch, and Goldbaum plowed on. "We face a budget crisis and possible cutback in services, including police enforcement. I'd like to propose a bill, rewrite, amendment or anything else to help on two fronts." The DA leaned forward. "Under present law the seizure of a vehicle, home, building is released with a fine. I'd like to tighten the noose. We'd disrupt crime by taking their property and create much-needed revenues by auctioning them off."

"This is a gray area, especially homes; one person using the home to, say, deal drugs would endanger any family members innocently living there. People would be put out on the street. I don't know Lew; this could backfire," the mayor cautioned.

"I understand the concerns, so what about limiting it to cars, boats, planes?"

"Uhm, transportation vehicles are something I think we can agree on."

"Excellent. One more thing though. I'd like to avoid the public hearings; we can't be tipping anyone off."

The lawmakers shook their heads and frowned, but they were no match for Goldbaum who was supremely prepared.

"Perhaps we can insert this seizure revision in the import statutes. Remember the case on Long Island where they used a fishing boat…"

The task force began adding interdiction patrols at the bridges leading into New York, stopping vehicles they believed suspicious. It took a few weeks, but eventually they began to make seizures. Though they averaged five vehicle confiscations a week, it just dented the flow of illegal smokes. Even more frustrating was the fact that none of the drivers would utter a word. The police would get the cigarettes. The driver would pay a fine, and that would be it. It was a big joke. They hoped things would change when the tougher law went into effect the following week.

Yuri popped out of the car and grabbed a briefcase from the back seat. "Don't feek around. Make drop and get back. I'm not gonna be long."

Yuri surveyed the area as he walked up to the front door and rang the bell. He heard Josephine as she came down the stairs.

"Hi, Yuri. Come in. Come in. He's in the kitchen finishing lunch."

"Good, so he's feeling good, no?"

"Ah, it's touch and go but he looks forward to seeing you each week."

They went up to the kitchen which overlooked the manicured backyard.

Yuri was surprised how feeble and gray Louie looked. "Bossman, how you doing?"

Louie cleared his throat and pushed a bowl away. "Yeah, some boss, eating fucking baby food."

Yuri put the briefcase behind Louie and shook his hand. "Yuri get you some borscht. He can have it, no?"

She cleared the table. "Ah, sure. Why not. Sit, sit. You want something?"

He shook his head. "Nyet."

Yuri sat across from Louie and struggled to hear him as they attempted small talk. Josephine finished loading the dishwasher.

"Okay, boys. I'll be downstairs if you need me."

Yuri moved to the chair beside Louie. "Got small problem. These feeking police, now they take cars and we lose 'em for good."

"What? Did you go to Johnny?" Louie referred to their lawyer, Johnny Apsco.

"Yeah, they changed law. He says they putting pressure on."

Louie hacked away, spitting into a napkin. "So, how many they get?"

"Three this week."

"Shit, that costing us like ninety grand. What the fuck we going to do?"

"Use old cars. If take, no big deal."

"Right, right. Go see Vic on Forest Ave. by the hospital; he's the best mechanic around, and he keeps his mouth shut. He can make a shitbox run like a Ferrari."

Yuri nodded. "He working on two already."

"Right, right. You got things handled? Huh?"

"No worry. Get better, okay?"

"Yeah, yeah, but if I can help you, if you need anything from me…"

"One thing: talk to that Sal."

"What? What's Sally doing?"

"Eh, he breaks my balls every time, always make challenge…"

"Sally's a good guy. We grew up in Brooklyn together. Leave it with me."

Chapter Nineteen

Yuri Popov operated out of a strip mall on Richmond Avenue. near the Staten Island Mall. Half of the retail space was taken by a large boxing gym and the balance filled with the usual suspects: a pharmacy, cleaners, pizzeria and liquor store. Yuri owned the gym called Gladiator Boxing and used a series of rooms above the gym as headquarters for his activities.

A heavily tattooed gorilla was glued to the camera feeds. "Hey, Ivan. I think your boy, he is here. Look."

Ivan checked the camera shot. "That's him. Let him in."

The door opened, and a wiry Hispanic walked in and was dwarfed by Yuri's men. They patted him down and handed him off to Ivan. "He's clean."

Ivan led him up a flight of stairs to an office outfitted with red velvet drapes and gaudy furnishings.

Yuri was behind his desk enjoying a plate of boiled potatoes and smoked fish. "Ah, Domingo. How you my friend?" He made no attempt to shake his visitor's outstretched hand.

"Good. READY to do business, Yuri?"

"Easy, my friend. Tell me again your plan."

Domingo fidgeted in his chair. "We went through it all; nothing's changed. Don't worry."

"Misunderstandings, they ruin many friendships." He roared with laughter and quickly quieted, staring at his visitor. "Tell me again."

"If you're getting cold feet, I got others that want in."

Domingo made a move to get up, and Ivan put his big mitt on his shoulder as Yuri said, "We get off on wrong foot. Maybe we start over, no?"

"Sure, sure." He leaned forward. "Like I said, my brother in law, he's in Miami, been dealing for a few years and does all right. He's got a solid connection for some high-grade shit coming out of Columbia."

"He bringing in direct?"

"No, no. He gets it from a guy he went to school with, but we could do it ourselves. I know it."

"Nyet, too complicated." He beckoned with his hand.

"So, like I was saying, we got solid supply, but my brother in law, he's lazy, doesn't want to expand. He's small potatoes; me I got big plans."

"So, if we give money, how you move the goods?"

"Don't you worry. I got more people wanting than I can fill."

"Yuri don't worry. He gets what's his." Yuri looked through his visitor.

Domingo shifted in his seat. "No, really. I've got a lot of ways to move it; I even got an NBA connection that if the quality stays where it is, we can push, and those guys snort like motherfuckers."

"Keep low profile, no like attention."

"Sure, sure. Whatever."

"So, you got everything, why you need Yuri?"

Domingo crossed and uncrossed his legs. "I, I, it's a cash buy. These guys, they won't front me credit. Got to give 'em dead presidents for the goods."

"What's number?"

"Well, I figure I get sixteen keys, I can buy at a little over twelve thousand a kilo, so I need about two hundred K."

"You said you sell for twenty thousand a key the other night."

"Yeah, yeah. That's right, maybe a little more." Domingo leaned forward.

Yuri rolled his chair back and put his feet on the desk. "The market's thirty a key; why sell below?"

"Uh, that's an estimate. If we can get more, all the better. We're splitting it down the middle."

Yuri rubbed the back of his head and shook his head no. "Get eight kilos, I'll give you hundred grand."

"But I told my source…"

"I don't give shit! Now, I don't want partner. I give a hundred; I get two hundred back."

Domingo looked from side to side, struggling with the math. "But that's, uh, it only leaves me with forty or fifty."

Yuri stood. "That's deal; you in or out?"

"I, uh, okay, but the next one…"

Yuri waved him over to the window. "Come. You see that?"

"The dump?"

"You know you can see from space?"

Domingo tilted his head, and Yuri, eyes narrowed, said, "You fuck with Yuri, and you go there. Understand?"

"Yeah, yeah. Trust me; you got nothing to worry about."

"Keep that way. Now sit."

Ivan put his hand on Domingo's chair, and Yuri left through a rear door into a den with a seating area and TV on one side and a large buffet along another wall. He pulled the buffet away from the wall, stepped behind it and unlocked it. Yuri opened the top, revealing an eight foot- by two-foot cavity that was four feet high and half filled with neat bundles of hundred-dollar bills.

A hand-drawn red line about three quarters of the way up lined the cavity. Yuri paused and fretted that between the cash going out to support his stable of boxers and declining revenues from cigarettes, his cash stash had fallen below his security line.

He reached in and dug out twenty bundles from a corner and locked the safe up. He set the bundles in shoeboxes and pushed the buffet back against the wall. As he carried the boxes out he calculated how many Miami trips it would take to cover the red line again.

Chapter Twenty

I was looking forward to a weekend of skiing up at Hunter Mountain. It was just going to be me, Phil and Joey. We were die-hard skiers, but sometimes a whole crew would come up, making the weekend focused more on partying than flying downhill. When it was only us three we always took it easy Friday night, ensuring we were in shape to enjoy the mountain Saturday. If a pile of friends came, essentially to party, it made it much tougher, and we'd have to step over them as we left in the morning.

I was getting my stuff together Thursday night when Tommy called.
"Skins, what's going on?"
"Fuckin nothing. You still heading to Hunter?"
"Ah, err, yeah, just me, Philly and Shem."
"I think I'll take a ride."
"It just us, you know."
Tommy sighed. "I need a fucking break."
"Oh, we'll have to take two cars; Shem was squeezing in the back of Philly's car."
"You can come with me," he offered.
"Uh uh, I got my snow tires on. We'll take my 280Z."
I pulled up to Donna's apartment, popped the trunk and rang the bell.
"Hey, Donna, how you doing?"
"Good, Vinny. Come in. It's freezing. I don't know how you guys do that skiing stuff."
"It's nothing if you dress properly."

As if on cue, Tommy came out of the bedroom with a duffel bag, wearing a thin leather jacket, jeans and sneakers.

"Like I said, dressed properly. Bro, you're gonna freeze your butt off."

"Don't worry about me, Jean Claude Killy."

"Tommy, why don't you take your pea coat?"

He shook his head.

"The news said it was gonna be way below zero honey. Come on, take it."

"Come on, let's go!" He barged past me without saying goodbye to Donna.

"See ya later, Donna."

She wore a sad smile and said, "He's one moody bastard; please bring him back with a smile."

He threw his bag in the trunk, and we jumped in the car. "What's up your ass?"

"Nothing. Stop at Willowbrooks. I gotta get some brews for the ride."

Tommy came out of the liquor wholesaler with a case, and before we hit the NY State Thruway he knocked off a six pack. He kept pretty quiet, and we talked about what trades the Yankees should make but not much else. We made a pit stop at exit sixteen, and he was more than half in the bag.

"Can't hold it like you used to, huh?"

"Not the brews; I had a lude or two." He slurred.

We were an hour into the weekend, and I'd have to figure out what was going on if I was going to enjoy the skiing, otherwise I'd end up playing Daddy again. We took a piss, grabbed some pretzels and hopped back on the thruway as it started to flurry.

"Hey, that's Joey, isn't it?"

"Yeah, that's the wanka."

"It's Wenkel, not wanka."

He pulled the tab on another beer and garbled, "Whatever."

I sped up behind him, flashed the brights, and Joey pulled into the right lane. We rolled down windows and shouted greetings at eighty miles an hour. When Tommy tried to pass a beer to them through the windows, I pulled ahead and hit the window button.

"You're fucking nuts, bro."

"What's the madder? 'Member we did it on the bridge that time?"

"The weekend just started. WE ain't even up there yet. Take it easy, will you?"

He sat quietly for a minute, then guzzled the rest of the can and reached for another.

When he popped it open, I said, "You want to tell me what's going on?"

"Nothing," he mumbled.

"Nothing? You're in a race to finish a case of beer." I looked at him. "On top of how many ludes,: two, three?"

He tilted his head to the window and flashed me two fingers.

"Slow it down, man; I'm going skiing, not to a hospital. What's eating you? You can talk with me, man. You can count on me; you know that."

He nodded and a barely audible whisper eked out, "Fucking pregnant."

I pulled in my chin and put both hands on the wheel. "Donna's pregnant?"

He nodded as I thought, *Oh, boy!* I scrambled to think and talk at the same time. Usually I could dispense what came across as sound advice but in the baby area?

I fiddled with the defroster. "It's going to be all right, Skins. Take it easy; you're not the first person to have a kid."

"I won't know what to do; it's gonna screw everything up," he muttered.

I recalled my dad's advice when I said I didn't want kids because the world was so screwed up that I wouldn't know how to keep my kids safe. He said, *"Just do what you know how to do."* I originally blew the advice off as stupid, but when I thought about it, it made complete sense. This, however, wouldn't work; simply repeating what he experienced would have similar results.

"Nah, it's something new. We can't be running around forever!"

He shrugged and took a guzzle. "I'm not the family guy, man. I don't know diapers and cribs and all that shit. It just ain't me."

"Bro, you complain, uh, sometimes about, you know, what you see happening in other families. This is a chance to do it right with your own kid."

He tilted his head. "I donno. The timing's just not right."

"Time's never going to be perfect; you know that. We got to play the cards we have."

"It sucks is all I know; not the kid, I mean. Donna's cool; she's right for me, I think, just too much at once, ya know?"

"Skins, one thing I know. We can't control it, the shit that happens, not all of it. Some of the crap is our own fault." I looked over at him, and he nodded in acknowledgment. "But what we can control is how we react. What we do when stuff happens, you know what I mean?"

"Yeah, I guess, but…"

"No buts, man. I didn't say it was easy, but sit on it, man. Don't get so down. Don't look for the easy way out." I looked at him. "No running this time, you hear?"

"I guess so, but now there's even more pressure to earn. On top of my mother and her shit, now I got to worry about a kid? And Donna's not gonna be able to work and…"

"Whoa, take it slow. Like I said, think, really think about it. We can talk it over. You know I'm there for you, man."

"Yeah, I know, man…thanks, but everything's upside down."

"After a week you'll be used to it. It'll be the new normal, you know?"

"Guess so."

"Listen, we got the weekend to bullshit about it. We'll work it out. Now cut back on the booze and change subjects."

We got to the rented house about eight o'clock, and as we unloaded the car Philly and Joey pulled up. The heat turned up, we left to grab something to eat. Tommy was making noise about going to the local club as we ate, but we wanted to get up in good shape, and since we had the keys, he could only grumble that we were old ladies. He fell asleep on the couch snoring minutes after we got back.

The rest of weekend he drank like a fish at times but seemed less reckless. We didn't have any real time to privately talk about his situation, but as we headed home his mood was brighter. During the ride we talked it over again, and I had the sense he had come to terms with the new responsibility he'd have.

Chapter Twenty-One

Goldbaum reviewed the latest data on the collection of cigarette taxes. It wasn't pretty; the downward trend hadn't budged since their initiative. He barked at an assistant to call an end of the day task force meeting before consulting with his chief of staff on strategy.

The room was full awaiting the DA as the sun sank below the skyline. New to the task force meeting was the Deputy Commissioner of Police William O'Reilly. The rising crescendo of chatter was quickly broken when Goldbaum entered the room wearing a forced smile.

"Gentlemen, thanks for coming on short notice."

He took a seat and continued, "New York is under siege, and it's vital that we do what is necessary to restore order." The comment raised some eyebrows. "This task force is an important element of our overall enforcement strategy. Paul, would you recap our activities?"

Paul Braddock, deputy of Strategic Policing, collected his thoughts. "Well, the main thrust of the effort has been observation and seizure. We've increased patrols at all port authority crossings and tripled the inspection rate. In regards to the seizures, we've had, geez, somewhere in the neighborhood of a hundred since we began with a value of contraband somewhere north of nine million."

"What's been the impact of the new forfeiture rule?" Lindenberry asked for the benefit of the other attendees.

"Well, since we've been taking the cars they move the cigarettes in, they've changed over to older, less valuable cars."

The DA's investigator, Ray Pirelli, shook his head knowingly. "The criminal element is an amoeba: it adapts."

Goldbaum got up and walked over to an easel, flipping over a large poster board. "We've got to change tactics, and we have to do it quickly. This graph represents the decline in tax revenues from tobacco. Unfortunately, the measures we've implemented have not even held the line."

Heads around the table nodded as he continued, "Let's put our focus on the sellers, bodegas, mom and pop shops, the convenience stores. They're the ones who are fencing the contraband."

"Good idea. If we reduce the number of outlets, prices will rise, less incentive to bring them up," Deputy Commissioner O'Reilly stated.

"I need, err, we need to reverse the loss of tax revenues immediately." Goldbaum sounded desperate.

Paul said, "I'll have my office get a listing of the stores with tobacco licenses. It's going to be a long one."

"First off, focus on the ones on the Island."

"And, at least initially, stay away from the 7-Elevens and chain stores. They're less likely to engage in shenanigans," Paul requested.

"Uh, I don't know about that, a lot of the 7-Elevens are franchised and controlled independently," Lindenberry countered.

"Good point. Okay, let's work with the list. Start on the Island and use some discretion. I'd say we direct each precinct to pay a visit, warn the owners about penalties for selling illegal smokes."

Goldbaum was rolling. "I'll have Al draft something on my office's letterhead that the officers can leave with the stores."

"Yes, but I want more than that. I want a police presence to be felt by the retailers, more drive-bys, more stop-ins, more…"

"We've got a limit on manpower, Lew," the police commissioner warned.

The DA frowned. "We all know a lot of crime emanates around these stores. We'd be executing our mandate to police the neighborhoods, and when this is done we'll have more resources to support the force."

"I will see what arrangements can be made in the morning's call with the precinct captains."

"Good, good. This is a high priority for the mayor. I've also spoken with Speaker Fineman. He'll introduce legislation to make it a felony to transport or sell contraband tobacco. Hopefully, these hoodlums will get the message when a few of the,,m are sitting in Riker's. Bob, can you take it from here and work out the details? I've got to run to an important press briefing."

Since there were only three precincts on Staten Island, the deputy commissioner made a conference call to the deputy inspectors in charge. Paul gave them the orders to put the heat on the retailers. Then he and the commissioner decided to also concentrate on Brooklyn and Queens, agreeing to have the patrol and organized crime units split up the turf, making stops at retail outlets to make their presence felt.

Back in his office, Goldbaum summoned his chief of staff.

"How'd it go, boss?"

"Excellent." He nodded. "We'll have every retail shop put on notice. I think it's the right strategy."

"But what about nailing Ruffino and the Popov? They'd be huge catches; we'd get tremendous press."

"I think we'll be able to make some hay either way. Crime is a big issue, but these days money gets the headlines."

Gordon raked his fingers through his hair. "True. How true."

"We know what the losses in revenue are, and we can truly point out when we stop it, how much we saved New York."

"Both state and city, we can use longer term projections for a higher impact. Headline effect."

"It's a solid issue; even smokers who benefit from lower prices know this is not good."

"So, when is the program going to roll out?"

"Right away, this week."

"Let me plant a few stories."

"I was thinking the surprise element?" Goldbaum dug out his lip balm.

"Not the way I see it." He made a frame with his hands. "We can have a couple of third-page stories headlining, 'DA Goldbaum moves to close illegal cigarette and protect NY tax stream…'"

Goldbaum leaned back. "Hmm."

"Either way, you get favorable press, and if the bodegas, that is if they even read the paper, see the stories it will help scare them."

Goldbaum's chief of staff received a raw feed of numbers on the tax collections and went to see his boss. He breezed past a secretary, knocked twice and stuck his head in.

"Lew, you got a minute?"

Goldbaum peered over his reading glasses. "Uhm, not really."

Gordon Black waved a sheaf of documents. "You've got to see this."

"Make it quick."

He sided over to the DA's desk and spread the sheets out. "It's been a month since we started pressuring retail outlets on the illegal smokes. But sad to say, it's having no impact."

"What? You mean to tell me the visits, the explicit warnings, are having no effect?"

"Zilch. Nada. Nothing."

Goldbaum sat back and pulled his glasses off. "This is a blatant disregard of the warnings; it is hard to believe. We sure we reached them all, issuing written warnings?"

"It's worse than that; the ones on Staten Island have been visited twice, and tax collections from the Island have actually declined!"

Goldbaum shook his head in disgust. "Not good. Not good at all."

"I don't need to remind you, boss; we've got an election coming up, and if we don't turn this around fast it'll be used against us."

Goldbaum nodded affirmatively. "I'll deal with it."

"You sure? Anything you need me to look after?"

"I've got it, Gordon. Now let me get back to what I was doing."

Gordon Black's footsteps had barely faded when Goldbaum picked up the phone.

"Hello, Raymond, hope I'm not disturbing you."

"Not at all, just getting my stretching in. What's up?"

"I'd appreciate it if you could gather some information for me."

"Sure. I could stop by tomorrow."

"This really can't wait. I, uh, we need this yesterday, so if you can get moving now, I'll provide details."

"Sure, boss. Fire away."

Boris sat in a small room at a metal table. He nervously scanned the stark room, focusing on the mirrored window. Jittery was an understatement, one second, he'd tug at an ear, then scratch his arm and rub his eyes as he shifted in the plastic chair.

Outside the window, Assistant DA Turbow and a detective watched him squirm.

"How long has he been in the room?"

The detective answered, "Fifteen minutes, tops. You want to go in?"

"Nah, let him stew a bit more. Come on, let's grab a coffee."

They sipped their java and watched Boris. When he laid his head on his arms Turbow instructed, "Time to go."

When the door swung open Boris nearly jumped out of his skin.

"Mr. Medev, this is the assistant DA, Ron Turbow."

"Assistant DA? But I didn't do anything. I'm just a small businessman."

"Easy, Boris. May I call you Boris?"

"Yes, yes. I don't understand what's going on. The detective said to come in for questioning, but I need to go back to work. My…"

"Don't worry you'll be fine if you cooperate."

Boris mouthed the word cooperate as the DA pulled a chair out and sat. "You sell a fair number of cigarettes at your establishments, don't you, Boris?"

He hesitated a split second. "Yes, yes, but we sell many items: food, drinks…"

Chapter Twenty-Two

Luqman parked his car in the condo lot off Forest Avenue and was making his way to his apartment when a loud crash sounded out. He snapped his head around and saw yet another accident at the dangerous intersection. This time it was an older car that had been mangled by a sanitation truck. He jogged over to help, as doors and windows opened to check out what happened.

The burly driver of the truck was trying to open the car's compressed door.

"I didn't see him! He came out of fucking nowhere. Help me! Over here, pull the door!"

They tried to pry it open but it was useless. Luqman peered in at an unresponsive, slumped body. He thought he recognized the scrawny, thirtysomething male but couldn't place the bloodied face.

"Maybe we can pull him through a window."

Luqman circled around the car, looking at an interior strewn with small, white paper bags. When he heard sirens he said, "I don't know; he looks bad. Let's wait till help gets here."

A fire truck and police car were the first to arrive, and they went to work cutting open the car as an EMT and more cops arrived. The sanitation driver was questioned by police as the driver was pulled out. EMT workers attempted to revive him but the doctor declared him dead. The corpse was quickly put in a body bag, taking an ambulance ride to the morgue.

Police photographers snapped pictures of the crash, measuring skid marks as Luqman lit a cigar and shot the shit with his neighbors. When a tow truck pulled the death trap away, onlookers retreated to their homes, shaken but resolved in the fight to improve the intersection.

At the racetrack the next afternoon, Luqman overheard a couple of stable hands talking and realized why he thought he recognized the man who died in the crash. The victim was Viktor Reshenko, a groom who'd started working at Aqueduct about eight months ago. Luqman didn't know him but felt terrible as he recalled the crash scene. He shook the image of a slumped Reshenko out of his head and made his way to Paddock Park to grab a brew with a buddy before the races.

Interstate 95 was dead; I pushed it a bit as I made circles with my left foot to stop it from falling asleep. I hit Virginia just before the sun and commuters made their appearances. Anxious to get home to Donna, I was doing five to ten miles over the speed limit when I noticed a trooper hiding. I slowed it down gradually by putting it in lower gear. It's never a good idea to flash your brake lights, and kept my eye on the rearview mirror. When a pair of headlights curved onto the road, I took a deep breath, signaled and moved to the center lane.

The fucking cop's lights were growing from pinpoints into dimes in the left lane. I grabbed a can of Coke and took a good swig. Fishing out the bennies in my pocket, I put them into the can, swirling it to help them dissolve. Then I kept it steady, hands at ten and two as the cop pulled behind me.

A sign stated the next service area was four miles ahead; I debated whether to pull in if he hadn't pulled me over by then. My mind was screaming for him to make up his fucking mind already, when he hit the strobe lights. Shit, now what?

I put on my blinker as the cop sped up, wondering how this would end up. Trying to recall the way Virginia troopers handled it, I moved to the right lane. Suddenly, the cop swerved left and sped past me. Fuck you, asshole!

Before I had a chance to settle down, I thought I heard a faint thumping sound. I shut the radio and it grew. Shit, don't tell me I've got a fucking flat! I slowed down and sure enough a damn flat was coming on fast. I put my flashers on and hoped to make it to the service area with some rubber left on the rim.

I had no frigging spare as about ten trips back, I starting taking out the spare and jack to fit an extra ninety cartons in. It gave me an additional hundred a trip but now it was payback time. I rolled past the rest area to a Sinclair gas station. One pumping station was open, but the service area was dark, so I pulled past the pumps to where the truckers grabbed some shuteye.

There was no one around, so I got out of the car and ambled over to the rest area. I took a piss and stretched before heading back to the car. I reclined the seat, adjusting the mirror, so I'd see when the repair area opened and tried to nap.

Awakened from truckers talking as they made their way for coffee, I noticed the green dinosaur sign was lit. I backed the car up to one of the bays and got out to talk to one of the grease monkeys.

"You're rolling on metal, man."

"I know my spare's no good. You got a tire for me? New or used, I don't care, just gotta get back on the road."

"Ah, think so." He bent down to read the specs. "Bobby, we got a two twenty-five by fifty, don't we?"

"Uh-huh, they'd be ninety dollars, plus mount and balance."

"Go for it, man."

He looked at the wheel. "Hey, I don't know about the rim, man. It's chewed up some."

"Don't seem too bad to me. I just got to get back home."

"Where's home?"

"Ah, Jersey."

"But you got New York plates."

"Look, my mom's not well, and I got no time. If you do it now there's an extra twenty for you."

"Hey, Bobby, the man's momma's sick. Get the jack and get moving."

I was back on the road in a half hour, and though anxious, kept a couple of miles under the speed limit. This shit was getting old; I needed to find something else to do. Maybe a bar or a pool hall; I could do that. What would it take to open one? I ran numbers through my head, making wild estimates without a shred of data to support them. But what the heck, it helped the time pass quickly.

I was never so happy to see the rusting arc of the Bayonne Bridge come into view. We'd started to use the Bayonne more times than not since the cops started their crackdown. It was a little longer, and believe me, after all the driving you were antsy but hopefully safer.

Keeping my eyes peeled for any coppers, I headed over the Kill Van Kull's murky water and paid the toll. The coast was clear as I motored down the Willowbrook Expressway and got off on Victory Boulevard, making a left to a new drop place that Yuri set up.

Lugman pushed open the door to Manhattan Bagel, grabbed the *Staten Island Advance* and thumbed through it as he waited on his morning coffee and buttered bagel. On page three was a picture of the wreck with a headline that almost made him drop his coffee.

The headline blared: 'Man Dies in Crash, Car Laden with Drugs'

Images of the small paper bags focused in Lugman's mind. He pulled the paper closer and read through the small story. When the article mentioned that the victim lived in Heartland Village, Lugman grabbed his bagel and coffee, and hustled to his car.

As he sped over the Verrazano Bridge his gut and shaking hands told him he was onto something.

Chapter Twenty-Three

Lugman called the morgue to get Reshenko's address. *Bingo*, he thought, it was one of the apartments over the boxing club. He picked up the phone.

"Detective Perilli, please."

"Perilli."

"Craig, it's Lugman. How you doing?"

"Good, Jack. What's up?"

"Need some information on that car in the wreck by my house."

"What do you need?"

"Can you tell me who it's registered to and where?"

"Yeah, sure. I'll get right back to you."

"Hold on a minute. I need something else. The car, it was found with drugs. I saw it myself, well, not the drugs but a bunch of, like, prescription bags. What drug was it?"

"Why you so interested?"

"Just a hunch, but if my gut's right, and it hasn't failed me yet, I'll drop it in your lap."

He hung up and went to see the editor of the business section. John Messina was hunched over a desk laden with annual reports and spreadsheets.

"Hey, Johnny, got a minute?"

He looked up and waved him in as he exhaled cigarette smoke.

"You look busy; want me to come back later?"

"Nah, just looking into the new kid on the block, Trump. He's making a lot a noise for a young guy."

"Don't know him."

"You will. What's up?"

"Can you tell me who owns a couple of corporations?"

"Assume you mean small private C corps."

"Not sure on the C part, but yeah, some private corporations that own horses. I need to see who's behind them." He handed him a slip of paper.

"Depends on how sophisticated they are. You know, sometimes there's offshore holdings and a web of stuff. Some of it's legitimate, you know, lawsuits and all these days. I'll make some calls. If I'm lucky you'll know in a couple of hours. If not, and I got to send Benny down to dig it out, it'll be a day or so."

"Look, if you can also get the addresses, I'll buy you a dinner at O'Brady's."

Yuri watched his newest addition to his growing boxing stable, a promising southpaw with a lightning-speed jab. He now had more than two dozen ranked boxers and three of the best trainers working full time for him. Done with taking the best boxers available, regardless of the class, he'd now focus solely on heavyweights. Yuri knew the glory and money were with the sluggers. As he observed his lefty work out of a cinch, Ivan tapped him on the shoulder.

"Boss, got some info."

"Trouble?"

He nodded.

Yuri pointed to the front door.

They went into the parking lot where Ivan told him that a full-scale investigation was underway at Aqueduct. This dovetailed with the sightings of agents at the track a couple of weeks ago and meant he'd made the right call to shut it down. He told Ivan to keep close tabs on it and went back inside.

Walking around the gym, Yuri's mind drifted to his troubled cigarette operation. The cash flow was drying up as the authorities ratcheted up the seizures and surveillance of his buyers. Since the pushback started, drivers wanted triple the price, and they'd lost a ton of cars and outlets to sell to. It just wasn't lucrative anymore. He'd also learned from police contacts that the DA was gunning for him at full speed. He thought over getting out of it, maybe turn it over to one of his guys and take a cut as long as it lasted. With the racing scheme also shut down, he needed an angle to replenish his cash pile.

He sat on a trainer's stool and tried to plot his next move. The money was good on the drug deal he thought, but it carried bigger risks, even fucking Apsco warned he couldn't help him if things went bad. Still, the margins were incredible, and if he wholesaled it, he thought he could keep a tight circle. He reviewed his holdings: strip joints were steady producers but they came with wheelbarrows of problems, and boy was he sick of problems. Loansharking was doing okay, but the gambling was maxed out and had high overhead. He rubbed his eyes, watched the newcomer on the heavy bag a few minutes and retreated to his office.

Yuri Popov sat alone in his office, and as classical music wafted through the air he continued to strategize. He tossed another empty Pepsi can into the trash, swung his feet off the desk and opened the door.

"I need Grigory."

He shut the door and went to the freezer, pulling out a bottle of Stolichnaya. He grabbed two shot glasses, and before he sat down there was a knock on the door.

"It's me, boss."

"Come, sit." He poured two shots and raised his.

"Here's to a good trip."

"Trip?"

Grigory had made two of three contacts that Yuri had set up when he heard the news that Boris had been brought in for questioning. Based on how things were going in Miami and what seemed to be more heat in New York, maybe they'd move south he thought.

The salsa music pulsated as Grigory surveyed the bar. He took a seat and couldn't keep his eyes off a red-sequined dancer as he nursed a scotch until his Hispanic contact arrived. They walked out into the humidity and drove to the waterfront where they talked business.

Though the monastically furnished room was cool, Boris had big wet rings under his arms. "I am an honest, working man."

"Look, Boris, we've got the transcripts. We know every single butt you bought over the last five years. It's clear you've reduced your purchase of legal cigarettes over the last twenty-eight months."

Boris scanned from man to man. "Uhm, I, I don't sell as much; business is not so good."

"Really, Boris? You've expanded quite a bit, no?"

He pushed his shoulders back a nudge. "I do what I must to survive."

"I guess that includes buying and selling contraband cigarettes."

"No, no I sell many, many products."

"Look, we can get the IRS involved; you do get a lot of cash, don't you?"

"Or the immigration authorities involved. There's a hearing coming up soon, I hear, for…"

Boris hung his head. "Ah, come on, guys: my mama, my sister? You're going after them. Leave them alone. They have a right to come to America."

"Like you said, Boris. We do what we have to."

"Listen, this can be easy, no problems for you or your family. We need you to cooperate in our case against Yuri Popov."

"Who?"

The two detectives looked at each other. "This guy thinks we're stupid."

"No, no, I don't really know this man, Yuri."

"Really, guess we must be mistaken or something."

"Maybe, yes could be."

"Then can you explain this?" He opened a thick file of photographs of Yuri and Boris, talking, shaking hands, sharing a drink, all at Boris's place of business.

Boris slumped in his chair. "Okay, okay. I know him, but please, I don't want to be involved. He can be dangerous, I hear."

"Too late for that, Boris. You're in up to your eyeballs now."

Chapter Twenty-Four

Lugman threw up his hands. "I don't understand how this affected the horses. What I remember about exercising, what little I did, was the soreness came the next day or so."

"Yes, normally that's right. You see, when we perform strenuous activities we breathe faster to get more oxygen to our muscles. But when, say, a sprinter, or in this case, a horse requires more energy than can come from aerobic methods, which is using oxygen, the body shifts to anaerobic energy production."

"Doc, you're losing me." He leaned in.

"When you need a burst of energy your body gets it by converting glucose into something called pyruvate."

Lugman rolled his eyes. "For God sakes, just tell me how it works!"

"Bear with me a second. Once the demand for energy ends, say, the end of a race, the pyruvate that came from the glucose gets converted to lactate. This happens over a day or so and produces that burning sensation in our muscles."

"But…"

He raised a hand. "This drug Baracodine dramatically speeds up the process and amplifies the burning or pain."

"Wouldn't this show up in blood or urine though?"

"I don't know if they screen for it, but any trace would be infinitesimal: the body burns it up."

Jack pondered and smiled before getting up, "Brilliant. You got to hand it to them, simple but effective. Got to go, Doc. I owe you a nice lobster dinner."

Back at the office, Lugman grabbed a cup of coffee and headed to the newspaper's huge library, pulling two thick volumes out.

He set the books on a table, took a sip of coffee and paged through the *Pharmacology Reference Book*. Lugman located Baracodine and learned it was made by Merck. He cross-referenced it to the manufacturers' index and wasn't surprised to discover the plant was in Linden, New Jersey. He jotted down the address and picked up the phone.

"Perilli, it's Jack. My hunch is playing out. The drug they're using is made in Linden. A hop and skip over the Goethals. What do you say we take a ride and check into this?"

"Into what?"

"I'm telling you that Yuri fellow is involved. The driver with the drugs lived in his building, and he worked at the track. Now we got a lead on the supply."

"You done playing detective, Lugman?"

"Come on, let's take a ride. This is gonna be big."

"No go, Jack."

"You don't believe me."

"Don't matter, little thing called jurisdiction, Colombo!"

"But…"

"Look, Jack, you've had your fun playing detective, so either give me what you got, or I'm going to hang up. I've got a desk full of cases."

Lugman, his disappointment evident, explained what he knew about the scandal.

My mother's sister had come in from Italy for the funeral: what a waste of time and money. The two of them, dressed completely in black were sobbing at the casket. I put my arm around my mom's shoulder and looked at my father, tempted to slam the top of the overpriced casket down and get this bullshit over. I didn't feel a thing, no emotion or anything. In fact, besides seeing my mom upset, I was kind of relieved he was dead. He was a terrible role model, and he put my mother through hell. Frig him, I thought as the first visitors crept into the room.

I had tried to convince my mother to cut the wake down to only two days, but the influence her old school sister had on her put me in a suit for three days and further into hock. The fact that my father didn't have the money to bury himself wasn't a surprise.

The funeral was a real charade. Every visitor said the rote bullshit they say at every wake: sorry for your loss, he was a good guy, blah, blah, blah. Even Yuri, who despised Billy, came and uttered empty nonsense. Two weeks before he kicked off he couldn't have borrowed a twenty from anyone. Now he was going to be missed? I couldn't wait till this crock of shit was over with.

The Mass was well attended, but the procession to Moravian Cemetery was just a few cars. After yet another ceremony we tossed some roses on the casket and headed for lunch at Carmine's.

I watched my aunt and mother bullshit away from the bar. Though they only saw each other every two years or so, they were tight. It was good she had her to lean on.

They were both mortified when the news we were having a baby out of wedlock came out. To calm them down I told them some bullshit that we were making plans to get married. The tale was more than enough for them to make a big fuss over Donna's pregnancy. It was great because Donna really loved the attention. A grandchild in the wings made for a great distraction, and I knew my mother would be able to move on with her family's support.

Chapter Twenty-Five

On the way to see my uncle, who'd been rushed to the hospital, I turned the dial to WINS 1010 looking for the results of the Lakers game I'd shut off in disgust. The Knicks had been down by twenty in the third quarter, and I kissed away the five hundred I had riding on them.

Heading down Forest Avenue, I thought about Louie and what seemed to be an ugly ending for him as I waited on the sports report. Deep in thought about the sorrow my mom felt and now my aunt, who had what seemed like a good marriage, I caught a piece of a headline about a scandal at Aqueduct.

I pulled into the hospital lot and waited for the headlines to cycle again. Sure enough, the newscaster announced that a probe had begun into possible race fixing at the Queens racetrack.

There were no more passes for his room, so I got the room number and went up through the emergency room. My aunt, Duke, Angelo and Carlo were all in the hall outside the room.

"How's he doing?" I kissed my aunt.

"Having trouble breathing. They're working on him now." She dabbed at her eyes as I shook hands with the others.

"Don't worry, he's tough."

A nurse popped her head out. "He's looking for you."

My aunt scurried in the room, and Duke leaned over. "Not looking good, man. Poor bastard's choking on his own saliva."

"Shit. Can't they do anything?"

They all wagged their heads and looked at their shoes. We remained silent, straining to hear what was going on the room. As a food cart passed I leaned over to Duke.

"I heard something's going down at the track. What do you know?"

He looked both ways and pointed me down the hall. As we walked he explained.

"They're onto it; that's why Yuri put it on ice."

Damn, I thought. The one thing I could count on was really dead. "Does Louie know?"

He nodded his head, and we headed back to the room.

Lying in the hospital bed, Louie looked like hell. He was on oxygen and had an IV bag and another wire or two coming out of him. It was eerie. I kissed his cheek and sat in a chair as a doctor came in asking for my aunt. She stepped into the hallway, and I watched as she talked with him. She put her hand to her mouth and leaned on the doorframe as the doctor left.

I went to her and put my hand on her shoulder.

"What's the matter?"

"Doctor said he's gonna need a tracheotomy." Tears streamed down her face.

A fucking trach? He'd be talking through a thing that made him sound like a robot? Holy shit! I thought, then asked, "They going to do this now?"

She shook her head. "Not now but soon I guess. You know how these doctors talk, never give you a straight answer." She began crying again.

"Take a walk, Aunt Jo. He can't see you like this."

The energy and hope were sky-high as fight night arrived. The winner of the Quarry-Lyle match would get a shot at Ken Norton for the heavyweight championship. The match was hyped with Ron Lyle, an ex-con convicted of murder going up against Jerry Quarry, the only white boxer ranked in the top twenty heavyweights. If Quarry won, the Great White Hope would fight Norton for the chance to be the only white champion since Rocky Marciano.

The area around Madison Square Garden was a zoo, thousands streamed toward the entrances as vendors plied their wares. The police kept the peace, shooing the panhandlers away and separating the highly charged fans when trouble erupted.

Yuri and his entourage were finishing up in Rivera's dressing room, three levels below the ring as Jack Lugman held his press badge up. As he went through the turnstile he ran into Charlie Bauer who covered politics for the *Daily News*.

"Chucky, didn't know you were a boxing fan."

"Well, truth be told, I'm not."

"Oh, covering fights of a different nature?"

He laughed. "That's good, Jack. Got a call from one of Goldman's lieutenants."

"What? Goldman, the DA?"

"Yeah. Hey, look, I really got to take a piss; I'll meet you in the press box."

The first match of the night had just gotten underway as Yuri and his boys settled into ringside seats. The place was filling up as the young welterweights danced their way through eight rounds, ending in a disappointing draw. Rivera was fighting in the third of six undercards, and Yuri knew the place would be jammed when the bell rang for his fighter.

The next fight ended quickly with a knockout in the second round. Yuri went to his fighter's corner as his boxer made his way down to the ring, and the crowd roared its approval of the hometown boy. Rivera, outfitted in red satin trunks and a matching hooded robe emblazoned with Gladiator Gym in black, waved to the adoring crowd.

Yuri beamed as Rivera hopped over the ropes and shadowboxed around the ring. He danced over to his corner where, Gus, his trainer and Yuri barked instructions as the announcer set up the bout.

"Pound him with the hook; don't let him pin you on the ropes. Roll away."

Gus put his mouthpiece in and finished with, "Make us proud, kid. You knock this fucking bum into next week, you hear?"

Rivera bounced on his toes and nodded. His eyes had the warrior look: intense but detached. The warning bells clanged, and he went to the center of ring to greet his opponent. The ref shouted out ground rules as Yuri made his way back to his seat.

The fighters went to their corners, and the opening bell sounded, sending them warily toward each other. Rivera flicked a couple of harmless jabs, and Floyd responded with a left cross that just missed. Rivera tried to paint Floyd into a corner, but though he might have been washed up, he was still fluid and turned him around. The fighters were feeling each other out, and as the round drew to a close the only shot that did any damage was a left hook Rivera landed as the round ended.

Rivera, skin gleaming with a thin coat of sweat, stood as a corner man applied Vaseline, and Gus pep-talked him. "Looking good, kid. Keep moving; cut the ring down; let him work. Use the jab. He's vulnerable, but watch out for his hook. He's still dangerous. You got it? Look, in a clutch, pound his ribs. You hear me? Pound them!"

Rivera who wasn't breathing hard, nodded nonstop.

"Okay, pulverize the bastard!"

The bell rang, and the fighters circled toward the center. Floyd threw a few jabs and Rivera backed up. Floyd crowded in and clutched Rivera who began to hit his ribs. Floyd muscled him into the ropes, and Rivera absorbed two hard hits before spinning away.

Yuri was on his feet yelling as Rivera started shuffling, showing off his footwork. Floyd seemed to slow down from the first round and threw a couple of roundhouses that never landed. The crowd liked the kid's showmanship, but Yuri winced; he didn't want the kid to appear cocky. He knew if Floyd landed a big punch, the kid's future would be over. Rivera faked left and right, landing a few jabs without impact. Floyd moved in, trying to clutch but Rivera spun away. The crowd roared as they mixed it up in the center, both of them landing solid punches as the bell rang.

The ref stepped in between and pushed them toward their respective corners as the crowd moaned its disapproval at the round's end. Suddenly, the crowd's attention turned to a contingent of police officers heading toward the ring.

Five uniformed officers were led by a pair of detectives, wearing dark suits and serious looks, down an aisle toward the ring. Heads followed the group as they made their way to the front row. The police scanned the expensive seats and pointed toward Yuri. Two officers guarded the aisles as the rest of the force got to Yuri's seats. Reaching into his suit jacket the taller detective spoke, "Yuri Popov?"

Yuri narrowed his eyes and nodded.

"Come with us. We have a warrant for your arrest."

The goons on either side of Yuri started to rise. Yuri grabbed both of their arms, and they sat back down.

"Warrant? For what?"

"Two counts of conspiracy, horse doping and gambling."

Chapter Twenty-Six

Turbow reported in. "We picked him up being processed at the fourteenth."

"Good, how did it go?" Goldbaum inquired.

"The Garden was mobbed, but we grabbed him in the middle of the bout, like you said."

"He start any trouble?"

"Nah, they say he was actually cooperative."

The DA quipped, "Yeah, well, Yuri's the type of guy who sends you flowers after his goons beat you to a pulp."

He chuckled. "Yeah, he's a sick one."

"See you in the morning, bright and early: my office."

Goldbaum came down for breakfast and smiled when he saw the paper's headline: 'Horse Race Fixing Ring Busted'

He turned the page and was pleased to see a stock photo of him next to one of the racing commissioner. He poured a mug of coffee and enjoyed the article over breakfast before heading downtown.

After attending the mayor's daily briefing and getting kudos, Goldbaum looked forward to getting to his office. He strode in, and the energy was palpable. A major arrest always charged the atmosphere with electricity, and this was a big one.

He said some hellos, dropped his coat and briefcase in his office and headed into the conference room.

"Good morning, gentlemen."

Almost in unison the salutation was returned by three men.

"Anything urgent out of the briefing?" Chief of Staff Gordon Black wondered.

"Just the usual pots boiling."

"Good, it'd be good to focus on Popov and his gang. I tell you, boss, this is going to poll well."

Goldbaum cringed. "We must be sure the public's trust in mutual racing is restored."

"Absolutely. We need to dig deep here; see what connections he and his group have. Just how widespread their tentacles go," Assistant DA Turbow offered.

Lindenberry, chimed in. "On it. I'm having the racing commish check for any patterns at Belmont and Yonkers."

"Good, good. We have to be aggressive, but don't go on any wild-goose chases. I want this highly focused."

"This Yuri Popov runs a tight ship. He's careful and calculating."

Turbow pointed a finger pistol. "Used to be Bob; we've got him in the crosshairs now."

"See what comes back. If it doesn't lead to anything concrete, we keep it to Popov," the DA instructed.

"It'd be nice to wrap it up quickly. A quick win would play well!" Gordon gave a thumbs-up as he got up. "Got to run to a campaign meeting." He headed for the door and looked back at Turbow and Lindenberry. "Don't tread on your Johnson gents; we've got an election coming up."

Johnny Apsco was already at the precinct reading the warrant and supporting brief when his client was brought in. While he was being booked, Apsco contacted the judge who'd signed the warrant. The lawyer made the case that with the business interests and property Yuri had, he wasn't a flight risk. The judge assured him that if Yuri surrendered his passport, he'd order his release pending a bail hearing.

Around midnight, an assistant delivered Yuri's passport to Apsco who promptly surrendered it for his release. The lawyer gave Yuri a wet towel to clean the fingerprint ink off and warned him to keep quiet as they exited the police station. As soon as they hopped into a waiting car Yuri asked, "How'd Rivera do?"

"Uh, he won: a knockout, I think."

"Can't believe I miss. Fucking pigs. They make Yuri pissed."

"It's Goldbaum, my contacts tell me. He's orchestrating it."

"Deal with it!"

"Yuri, this is a serious, high-profile case. That egomaniac Goldbaum is salivating over it."

"What are you trying to tell me?"

"It's early, but this could be a tough case. I hear they got a solid witness and—"

Yuri stiffened, "Witness?"

Apsco raised a hand. "Hold on, we're meeting with the DA next week. We'll hear what they got, and take it from there. Okay?"

Yuri grunted.

"Leave it to me; you lie low till we figure out what's going on."

I had missed two straight weeks of bowling and got to Coral Lanes early to shake the rust off. After I shot fifteen practice frames I went to get a soda and saw Tommy at the bar.

"Yo, Skins, how's it hanging?"

"Pretty fucked up if you ask me."

"What's going on?"

"Ah, my uncle sounds like an alien."

I tilted my head.

"They took his voice box, man. Now he puts a frigging mic up to his neck. It's spooky."

"I hear you, but at least he's alive."

"I don't know, man. He looks like an old man: he got no power. He's nothing but a lapdog for Yuri now."

"What do you expect, man? He's real sick."

"He should've handed it down, man,: kept it with the family."

"I don't know. Didn't he get sick fast…"

"But fucking Yuri? Man, he's not even Italian."

As his car pulled up in front of 80 Centre Street, Apsco wondered how the news that Goldbaum was running for mayor would play in the case against Yuri Popov. Goldbaum knew how to play the media but so did he. As he placed his alligator briefcase on a conveyor belt, he started to think a quick plea deal may be the best route. Yuri had no record and was adamant about keeping clean. Goldbaum could put a notch in his belt. It wouldn't be a big win, but he'd gotten good press on it and it would clear his calendar to campaign. He smirked as he got in the elevator thinking, after all, it was all about appearances for both men.

Both assistant DAs were standing, chatting when Apsco was shown in.

"Counselor, good to see you."

He extended his hand,

"Ron, Bob, you're both looking well."

Ron Turbow eyed his suit. "Not as good as you. What's that, silk?"

Apsco pinched his delicate tie. "Italians do make the finest."

"Business must be good."

"Can't complain. Let's get down to business, shall we?"

Lindenberry cleared a chair for Apsco and joined Turbow across the conference table. The prosecutors pulled out files, and Apsco responded with a yellow legal pad.

Apsco rolled his chair to the left, out of a stream of sunlight, and as he pulled a gold pen out of his jacket, offered, "For the record, Mr. Popov has various legitimate business interests and has never been convicted of a crime."

"We're more familiar with your client than you know. As for his business, hobbies or other interests, if they're illegal we'll put an end to his perfect record."

Apsco raised his eyebrows and pointed to the file. "Shall we?"

Turbow scrunched his chair closer to the table and opened the folder. "Okay, so our original charge was for gambling, conspiracy, use of illegal narcotics, doping of horses, and animal endangerment."

Apsco tilted his head. "I read the indictment but endangerment?"

"The horses could have injured themselves when they were drugged."

Apsco smiled. "You're reaching to lengthen the list of charges. Fair enough. What do you have for evidence?"

Lindenberry shifted in his chair. "While we're still doing discovery, we have enough evidence to convict on the fixing of at least four races."

"Really? Why don't we leave that up to a jury? What do you have?"

"We intend to show that Yuri Popov was the mastermind of a grand conspiracy to profit from a race-fixing scheme. Our evidence will show that he was involved in the obtaining and administering of drugs to horses racing at Aqueduct. That under his direction, the outcomes of at least four races were altered, and that he and his associates profited by placing large wagers, knowing in advance, the outcome. That such action not only undermines the confidence the public has in the racing establishment but is in direct violation of Code—"

Apsco raised both hands. "Geez, I didn't come here for an opening statement. How about the evidence?"

"For starters, we possess video footage of known associates of Mr. Popov making especially large bets on the races in question."

Apsco shook his head. "Circumstantial at best. These folks do have a history of playing the ponies."

"Maybe, but the groom, who we believe administered the drugs, wasn't only an associate of Mr. Popov's but lived in one of his buildings and drove a car registered to the defendant."

"You mean Victor Reshenko who, unfortunately, is no longer with us? How'd you get an arrest warrant with such garbage?"

Turbow smiled and looked at Lindenberry who responded, "Pretty easy, actually; we have a solid witness who was the conduit for the drugs and will testify."

Apsco felt himself flinch, wondering if they noticed. "Testify? Interesting. So, who is it?"

"Sorry, Counselor, no names till the last minute of discovery."

Apsco thrust forward. "What? He or she in protective custody?"

"We're not at liberty to disclose details."

Apsco put both hands on the table. "That's bullshit, and you know it!"

"The DA instructed us accordingly. If you don't like it, go see Judge Carlino."

"Damn sure I will. Is that your whole case?"

Turbow closed the file. "We're still developing but believe it's strong."

The defense attorney regained his footing. "Matter of opinion. You know I'd love to go mano a mano with Goldbaum in the courtroom, but don't know if I can stand the heat of all the TV cameras." Apsco laughed.

Turbow slid a file with a summary of the information across the table. The counselor signed a receipt and got up.

"What do you say we meet a week from Tuesday?"

Yuri and his attorney settled into a corner table at Carmen's Restaurant in Annandale. They had a drink, ordered appetizers and went out to the deck to talk where the breeze was fishy and laden with salt. Yuri offered his pack to Apsco who declined. As Yuri lit up the lawyer spoke, "Most of the case is circumstantial, and I'll rip 'em to shreds. But an area of concern is a witness."

"Who?"

"Don't know, but they say he acted at your direction to procure the drugs and will testify against you."

Yuri laughed. "Yeah, if he—"

Apsco raised a hand.

"Any ideas who it might be?"

He shook his head. "Yuri keep small circle."

"Direct testimony from an insider will be difficult to defend. This could get very messy, Yuri. The sooner we know what we are up against the better the outcome."

The defendant narrowed his eyes. "Yuri, check around."

"Okay, but please listen to me; don't do anything stupid, okay?"

Yuri nodded.

"Goldbaum's running for mayor; my hunch is they may be interested in accepting a plea bargain to a lesser charge."

Yuri quickly shook his head no.

"All I'm asking is to consider the possibility of say a six-month term for illegal gambling, rather than risking a ten- or twenty-year term."

Yuri took a long drag. "You see big ship out there? Yuri come on smaller, all the way from St Petersburg. I no cop plea to go in slammer. No, even one fucking day!"

Donna and her sister were at the kitchen table when I came in.

"Hi, honey."

"Hello, ladies." I headed to the fridge.

"Come here. Check these colors out."

The table was strewn with color sticks from the paint store. I took a swig of beer as Donna asked, "What you like best? We got to stay neutral."

I threw my coat onto the couch. "Whatever you want, as long as it's cheap. I got to shower, got a meeting."

"Meeting? With who?"

I glowered and headed for the bathroom. Showering, I wondered what Yuri wanted. He was tough, nah make that impossible, to read. The cigarette business was down big-time, but he seemed to be doing okay. It was the guys like me that were taking it in the wallet.

Opening the door to the Gladiator Gym, I was greeted with the hum of warriors getting their work on the speed bags. It sounded like a bunch of high-speed bean counters working adding machines. There was a crowd watching the newest heavyweight in Yuri's stable spar with one of two ex-pros who worked there. The kid was good, but the old professional found openings, making Yuri wince. He noticed me and whispered to Igor who ushered me up to a small foyer where a goon was glued to video feeds of the place.

After fifteen minutes, Yuri's door swung open and Igor stuck his chin out. "Boss is ready."

I was thrown off to see Yuri behind his desk, unsure how he got in there.

"Hey, Yuri, that kid looked pretty good."

"Eh, he green, Smokey slipped in whenever he wanted."

"Yeah, well. He'll learn."

"Sit." He looked to Igor who promptly closed the door behind him. "Everything good?"

"Yeah, okay."

He leaned back in his chair and stroked his chin. "I hope we don't have problem."

"No, no problems."

"Hmm, then when you pay?"

I was in the hole twenty grand, having double downed on the fucking Jets Sunday. "I know, but the last couple of months, my father passing, and I hardly been given any trips to make, and…"

He held up a hand. "No cry, when Louie cut you off, you come to me, no?"

I nodded.

"I say okay, but am I fool?" He pointed a finger at his chest.

"No, no."

Yuri raised his voice several notches. "You owe, don't pay and double down?"

I was pissed I put myself in this position with the commie. "I'm good for it. You know me, Yuri. Just give me a little time."

"Know you? Like you father? He owes me big! Now dead, what I get?"

It stung to hear it, but I agreed inside. "Don't worry."

"Ah, worry I do. Twenty points a week on twenty K is big hole."

"I'm working on a couple of things, could be some nice scores."

Yuri raised an eyebrow. "Tell me."

"Well, ah, it's early, but I got a line on some cameras coming in for Christmas."

He frowned. "Months away. "

I nodded.

"I have project, gift from Yuri."

A burn rose in my belly. What was this fucking Russian up to?

Yuri got up and put the TV on, raising the volume before sitting down next to me. He leaned over, and I could smell the anise liquor he liked with his coffee.

"I have special business, secret, understand?"

"Sure, sure."

"You good driver, smart driver. You drive two, three times, and Yuri wipe slate clean."

Yuri was short on details but was going to give me a package, which had to be cash, to take down to a contact in Miami. I'd get a parcel and head back up. He told me to come in very late the next night and be ready to leave straightaway.

He took out two shot glasses, filled them with vodka and shouted a toast in Russian.

My head was swimming; I trotted down the stairs and out the rear entrance to my car. Was he setting me up? Nah, that didn't make sense. Miami? Gotta be drugs, the fucking Columbians are all over the coke business down there. Was Yuri muscling in? Shit, these guys would put a fucking bullet in me in a heartbeat. Ten grand a run? Gift, my ass, it's dangerous. I was boxed in. Shit, if he didn't shut down the Aqueduct scam I could've made some scores, but now I gotta run smack?

Maybe I should bounce it off Vinny? Yeah, that's what I'll do. I felt a sense of relief at the thought of talking it through, but before I turned off Richmond Avenue I realized he'd talk me out of it, and I'd have no way to make the dough I needed.

Chapter Twenty-Seven

The meeting was tense; Apsco pushed to determine who the witness was, but the assistant DAs held their ground.

"Listen. All is fair in love and war, gents, but holding out till the last minute is only going to cause me to file motions to delay a trial. That is, if we ever have one."

"Carlino set the discovery time limit; at end of period we give you what we got."

"We can play it anyway you want. You'll argue that you complied with the time line, and I'll argue it was a material witness that you knowingly withheld. We'll go back and forth, and some compromise will be struck, giving me more time."

Turbow put his wrists together. "Our hands are tied."

"I see. Look, I may be able to convince my client to entertain a plea. Avoid the expense of a trial"—he threw up a hand—"to something like illegal sports wagering."

"You got to be kidding."

"No jail time, suspended sentence, with a hefty fine for the DA to feed to the press."

"Sorry, Counselor. Mr. Popov's going to have to do some time."

"Be realistic. Your case is highly circumstantial. You've got all your eggs in one basket with your mystery man."

"It's a steel basket."

"Hmm, he's in protective custody, then."

"The DA needs to send a message with this case; the public's confidence is at stake."

,"Come now, this is nothing but a show; you fellas got an election coming up."

"We have nothing to do with that."

"The fact is he'd love a big case to boost his image, but that comes with the risk of a long, drawn-out affair that may not go as well as his campaign would like."

"You have some pair, Apsco."

The defense lawyer pounded his finger on the table. "The fact is with a plea, he can get a win here and move on to campaigning while collecting some nice money for the government."

"Define nice money."

"I haven't flushed this out with my client but we'll make it substantial. Hey, maybe we'll even donate to his campaign." Apsco laughed heartily. "Let's say a quarter of a million."

"It's not going to fly without any jail time. Sorry, Counselor."

Yuri was up in his office talking with a trainer about the prospects of a new heavyweight in his stable of fighters.

"You know he's got good instincts, footwork is crude, but I'll get Vince to shape him up."

"Run him hard, get rated. Fight for bigger purses."

"He's a bit of a bleeder, Yuri."

"Use stuff that Demetri make?"

"Yeah, some magic concoction, it seems to be working, but we ran out yesterday. You see Demetri around?"

Yuri stiffened like a dog detecting an intruder, "Check pharmacy."

"They say he's not been in for a few days."

Yuri made inquiries about his hunch that Demetri Asimov was the mystery witness. Demetri, who ran the pharmacy in Yuri's shopping center, had been a helpful associate and reliable source of painkillers, skin-toughening goods and assorted pharmaceuticals for his boxers. Demetri, a sports trainer, who hailed from Ukraine, was well known in the Baltic region for his ability to get athletes back in competition quickly after injury. However, after being sanctioned by the Romanian Gymnastics Association that spawned other investigations, Asimov went on the run. Claiming the desire to be with his only sister, Valeria, Demetri immigrated to the United States and moved into a place Yuri owned.

Yuri went to see his sister, who operated a small seamstress business on Manor Road. He flipped the Open sign over, locked the door and walked over to Valeria who was hunched over a sewing machine.

"Ah, Valeria, has been long time, no?"

Startled, she pushed the jacket she was working on aside and got up. "Yuri, I, I, ah yes. Do you want café?"

He shook his head. "My Valeria, what are we to do with Demetri?"

Tears started to sprout from her eyes, and he said, "Sit, sit."

Valeria sat and stared at her lap while Yuri took the sewing machine stool and moved knee to knee.

"I hear that maybe Demetri he not loyal. Maybe misunderstand?"

She shrugged her shoulders.

"You go, tell him nothing to fear from Yuri. Who help Demetri when he came?"

She looked up hopefully and brushed a tear aside. "Yes, I am sure he knows."

"Go. Tell him important everyone's, uhm, how we say, wellbeing, he come see Yuri."

She sniffled as he patted her arm. "No worry; Valeria no worry."

Yuri stood, pressed five hundred dollars into her hand, told her to close up and go to her brother.

Turbow and Lindenberry debated who'd make the call to Goldbaum. They decided to reach out to his chief of staff, Gordon Black. Turbow picked up the phone.

"Gordon, it's Ron."

"Ah, Turbow, to what do I owe this pleasure?"

"Ah, there's been a, a development in the Popov case."

"Don't ruin my day, Ron."

"It seems Demetri Asimov's gone missing."

"Seems? What the hell is going on, Turbow?"

"We sent a car for him yesterday. You know, to prep him, but he was gone, and the black-and-white guarding the apartment didn't see him leave."

"Ah, geez, Turbow. Get your asses out and find him!"

"Yeah, we're sorry."

"Sorry don't cut it. Find him! And keep a lid on this; I don't want the press to know."

I checked the rearview mirror, fished the last cigarette out of the pack and tossed the wrapper out the window. A Welcome to Maryland sign flashed by as I lit up and thought, *Just out of Pennsylvania, and I'd I smoked a pack already?* Damn, I'd taken a circuitous route out, but I was smoking way too much. I slid down the rear windows of my Firebird, thankful I didn't need the space: taking my car would be a change of pace.

Sick of driving and this a longer ride to boot, I'd toyed with the idea of staying over a day on the way down, but since I was broke and had to pay for all the baby stuff I quashed it.

The music sucked. I needed distraction; I was thinking too much. The more I tried to figure things out the more confused I got. Bottom line was I didn't know what the fuck to do. I had a kid on the way and wasn't really sure how I felt about it. I just couldn't get roped into a life like the suckers in the neighborhood, working a measly job for a couple of weeks off a year and a new car every five years. What was the point? I couldn't see my way clear to be happy with that.

It'd be nice to be father to a son, play ball, show him the ropes, help him out and all, make him feel like he fit in. I could do that! I think. I tore open another pack of Marlboros. But me and Donna weren't married, and the kid should have a normal household, but last time I got hooked it was a disaster.

Making money, having a kid, being married, shit, nothing had an easy answer. I took a deep drag, exhaled and reached for the dial again.

The Latin section of Miami was jumping and just before midnight I drove by an Ocean Avenue. club where a bouncer in red pants sat outside the door. Multicolored strings of lights flashed as salsa music leaked into the night. I slowed down, circled around and parked a block away. When I turned the corner, the bouncer trained his eyes on me as I approached, not moving even though a loud Spanish couple spilled out of the club. The spic stood and followed me in. The joint was half full but the dance floor was jammed with grinding couples and saucy chicks.

I hopped onto a barstool, ordering a Black Label from a bosomy barmaid. When she delivered the drink, I yawned and asked her if Juan Carlos was in. She nodded and whispered to a bearded goon by the service bar. Sipping the scotch, I zeroed in on a dancing, red-skirted senorita, when a beefy man of about forty slid onto the next stool.

"Looking for me?"

"Alberto said to say hello."

He tilted his head toward a hallway and got up.

I followed him down through a door, into an alley where he knocked three times on a door of the next building.

"You got the money?"

"Yeah."

"Let's see it."

I smiled. "Come off it, man. You'll get it when we trade."

He eyed me. "Wait here." Then he disappeared.

The hand off was set for 5 a.m. at Yiya's Bakery on Seventy-Ninth Street, just off Biscayne Blvd. I circled in the dark past the brightly lit shop, before pulling in the lot. There were six cars belonging to the staff parked at the rear, and I took a spot close to the street. A sign said Closed but the door wasn't locked.

Place smelled great, and as an aproned baker carried in a pan of fresh bread, I thought of Louie and his Brooklyn bread supply when a leather-jacketed spic appeared.

He had a thin moustache and curly hair. He waved me over and quickly frisked me.

"You got the dough?"

I wanted to make a wisecrack but nodded. "You got the goods?"

He narrowed his eyes, and for a flash I thought he'd pull a blade out. I told him the money was in the car.

We went into a small storeroom where bags of flour and sugar were piled chest high. The Chicano reached into a barrel and came up with four packages. He grabbed bread wrappers off a shelf and stuffed them in like loaves of bread.

"Pull around back."

We quickly made the exchange. I put the goods in plain view on the back seat next to the cooler and headed for I-95 in the dark. I fought the urge to put the pedal to the metal as I climbed the ramp onto the highway. Cotton mouthed, I settled into the center lane and reached back for a drink.

I passed Cape Canaveral before the adrenaline rush dissipated and was calm, but by the time I hit St. Augustine I tired and needed a boost. I fished out a pair of uppers out of the glove box and washed them down with a mouthful of Coke. When the Georgia border came up I was wide awake and making good time. It was a bit before noon and being that the ride through Georgia was quick, I vowed not to stop till South Carolina for gas and a leak.

Interstate 95 was crawling with cops, and the traffic slowed as it wound through the Washington DC area. I kept in the middle lane as Virginia gave way to Maryland just before dinnertime. Delaware came up quick, and seeing signs for Jersey gave me a boost. I'd be on the Island in three hours.

As I crested the Bayonne Bridge I noticed two cop cars in the toll booth plaza and eased off the gas. *"Set-up"* screamed in my mind as I descended. I casually glanced over and saw the officers talking through the windows and eased into a middle toll lane. The stakes were higher, but the same old ghosts haunted me.

After calling Ivan from a pay phone, I headed to hand off the blow at a Laundromat on Victory Blvd.

Chapter Twenty-Eight

A green garbage truck scattered seagulls as it chugged to the top of Fresh Kills Landfill and waited for the truck ahead to dump its load. A sanitation worker waved him to back up as a backhoe finished spreading the last load of refuse. The driver put the tilt mechanism into play and watched the worker signal to inch forward, easing the load out. Suddenly, the worker waved his hands to shut it down. The driver hopped out into the stench, jogged to the back of the truck and froze as the worker raked trash off a naked, decomposing body.

The police arrived, along with the medical examiner who determined the death was due to multiple gunshot wounds. It was also noted that the middle-aged white male was missing his tongue. The trash the body arrived in was quickly traced to the South Beach projects, and an investigation into the homicide was launched as the body left for the morgue.

Except for the missing tongue, the Island's newspaper didn't play up the gruesome discovery at the world's largest dump. It was the third body found this year, and it was widely suspected that several more went undetected.

It took a few days for the stiff to be identified, but when Yuri was handed the *Staten Island Advance* he suppressed a smile at its headline: Tongueless Body Was Key Witness in Racetrack Scandal

* * *

Flanked by assistants, Goldbaum stood to the side of the podium as his press secretary began, "In our continuing effort to keep the public informed, I'll read a brief statement, and the district attorney will take a few questions." He cleared his throat. "Contrary to rumor, the unfortunate discovery of Mr. Asimov's body will not derail the Aqueduct case. This development does impact the case as Mr. Asimov was a powerful witness. However, this office believes we have enough supporting evidence to successfully try the charges against Mr. Popov. In closing, it should be noted that this office has opened a new investigation into the death of Mr. Asimov. We will determine the circumstances of his demise and pursue the disturbing possibility of witness tampering with vigor."

The trio of lawyers moved to the podium, and Goldbaum put his hands on it and smiled.

"I'd be happy to answer some questions."

A sea of hands went up, and Goldbaum pointed to a reporter who covered crime for the *Daily News*: Sammy DeStefano.

"My sources tell me the case against Popov relied heavily, almost exclusively, on the testimony from Asimov. How can you get a conviction without him?"

"Now Sammy, you know this office wouldn't indict anyone solely on the basis of one witness. We look for corroboration in each and every case. During this long investigation we have gathered other evidence that we believe incriminates the defendant."

"Are there other witnesses?" Sammy tried a follow-up, but the DA picked another reporter, Joe LiBecci from the *Staten Island Advance*.

"The public's confidence in legalized gambling is on the line." Goldbaum, a grave look on his face, nodded in agreement, as LiBecci continued, "So with the stakes so high, why was such a crucial witness not in protective custody?"

"The New York Police Department, for whom I have the highest regard, were responsible for monitoring the witness." Goldbaum called on another reporter, this time a friendly face from the *New York Post,* who surprised him.

"You didn't answer the previous question: why wasn't Demetri Asimov in protective custody?"

"It was decided that, although he was a highly regarded witness, that he was not in imminent danger. And let's not jump to conclusions that the case had anything to do with his demise."

The *Post* reporter quickly followed up: "But Asimov was a known associate of Popov's, who is, shall we say, of debatable character?"

"Please, let's not besmirch Mr. Popov's reputation; he has never been convicted of a crime. Frank, you're next."

"Thanks. You stated a moment ago, and I paraphrase: *it was decided*. Can you tell us who decided?"

"Uhm, well, that decision was in the hands of the assistant DA's; they made the call." He threw up his hands, quickly adding, "But I take full responsibility for the office."

"Since you're running for mayor, do you think this case has any political ramifications?"

"My responsibility is to defend and protect the citizens of New York. This office is and will remain above politics." He took a step back from the podium and finished with, "I am truly sorry that I don't have more time, but I have an important meeting with Mayor Price."

Goldbaum fibbed; he wasn't meeting with the mayor, but with his chief of staff, who ran the mayoral campaign. His forced smile turned to a scowl as he and Black went into his office.

The DA collapsed into his leather chair. "Is this what it's going to be like?"

"The higher up in office, the brighter the glare." Black fished out two sodas from the small fridge and handed one to his boss. "The timing sucks on this Popov thing. I'm thinking we need to take some action."

"Action?"

"Look, your guys blew it here. It may look good to let one of 'em go, shows you're in control, taking action…"

"What? Terminate Turbow or Lindenberry?"

"Lew, someone has to take the blame for failing to protect a high-profile witness."

"It's more complicated than that, Gordon." Goldbaum stood.

Black wagged a finger. "No, boss, it's really simple. It's either you take the hit or someone else."

Goldbaum nodded as he sat back down. "I know you're right, but I don't want my office taking responsibility. I want as much distance from this fiasco as possible. Besides, we had a damn patrol car sitting on the witness. If anyone should take the fall it's the police."

"Why don't we call Argento. He owes you a couple of favors."

Goldbaum pondered, then picked up the phone and called the police commissioner. After the pleasantries he swiveled his chair to face the window. The negotiations ended quickly, and the DA turned his chair around.

"He agreed to put the officer on paid leave."

"It'd be better if he were fired."

"Wouldn't go for it, said the union would crawl all over him."

"Okay, okay. We'll get this in the papers; it'll take some of the heat off, but what about the case itself?"

"Not good, we needed Asimov. He was inside the operation, and now unless we can link Popov to his death, it's going to be a tough case to try."

"Lew, we can't have an unknown. A loss in a high-profile case like this would be a disaster; the other campaigns will drag us through the mud."

Goldbaum clasped his hands. "I know, I know. I already authorized Turbow to negotiate a plea."

"Perfect. We'll make it look like a thirty-year sentence. Hey, make sure it includes a sizable fine. We'll get some mileage out of it."

Turbow shook Apsco's hand and settled in a comfortable chair in front of the lawyer's desk.

He swept his hand around. "Nice digs, Counselor."

"I like my clients to be comfortable."

He pointed to the full bar and seating area. "That's a heck of an understatement."

"You should consider private practice, Ron: no pension, but the pay grade is a helluva lot better."

Turbow shook his head. "Man, you ain't kidding."

"So, what's on your mind?"

"Off the record?"

Apsco nodded, and the assistant DA opened up. "Goldbaum's running for mayor and wants to clean the calendar for campaigning. He'd like to settle as many cases as possible."

"I'm all ears."

Chapter Twenty-Nine

After meeting with Apsco, Turbow went to see the DA.

"You're not going to believe it, but Apsco said he won't let Popov plead guilty to anything."

"Even without jail time?" Goldbaum cocked his head and reached for his lip balm.

Turbow shook his head.

"What about a fine?"

"Nope, said we don't have enough to move the case forward and wants the charges dropped."

Goldbaum drummed his fingers on the desk, "Dropped? So, we get nothing."

"He said, and I quote, 'We'll keep it quiet, no bad press for the DA, or if he likes, we can go for some headlines.'"

Goldbaum stroked his chin. "If Popov comes up clean in this Asimov business, I'll agree to a quiet ending. We're closing in on him in the cigarette case anyway."

With no concrete evidence that Yuri was involved in Asimov's death, the DA's office called Judge Carlino, telling him they would submit a motion for dismissal. They asked it be kept as quiet, but within hours the DA's office was besieged with calls for explanation. Their press secretary put out a statement that failed to satisfy the reporters, and the morning's papers featured the story.

The *New York Times* column was the kindest, noting that the case against Popov collapsed with the death of a material witness. The article put the blame on the police for failing to keep Asimov safe but raised the embarrassing question of why Goldbaum held a press conference to announce the indictment but looked to keep the dismissal quiet.

The *Daily News* ran a page-two story leading with a headline that read: 'Thin Case Against Popov Crumbles'

The three-column article rehashed the horse-racing scandal and questioned why, what they characterized as a flimsy case, it was brought in the first place. The reporter questioned the DA's tactics and featured an unflattering picture of a grim-looking Goldbaum.

Splashing the front page with what was easily the most damaging story, The *Staten Island Advance* headline read: 'DA Botches Racing Scandal Case'

The reporter placed the blame for failing to protect the witness squarely on the DA's office. The critique held the attorney general not only responsible for the failure of the case but just about convicted him of having a hand in the murder of Asimov. The commentary went on to question the core competency of the office's ability to keep the public's confidence.

It was a pit bull-like attack and finished with wondering if the episode would affect the mayoral race.

As if the article wasn't damaging enough, the paper followed the next day with a scathing editorial on the rise of organized crime in the city. Though it did not name Goldbaum, the basic premise of the piece was why any insider or whistleblower would come forward if the justice department could not guarantee their safety. It was a basic responsibility, that in the paper's opinion, the department failed miserably in.

The initial poll results after the articles hit Goldbaum's numbers hard. He fell to a distant second just barely ahead of an unknown councilman. Black and his mayoral committee instructed Goldbaum to stay in the public eye but out of the press's reach. They arranged for the DA to be present at three different drug busts by the feds as well as a handful of appearances with the governor and mayor. They made sure he was seen but not heard. Goldbaum's numbers stopped falling, but the real damage to his candidacy was done, and work to repair his image was needed.

Less than two weeks after the first Miami run I was back on I-95. After haggling with Yuri, he agreed that this run would get me even. Since I'd cut back on gambling, the truth was being cut off had a lot to do with it; the pressure had eased a bit. Almost out of the hole, I was upbeat, and with Donna days away from giving birth, I still didn't know if I was looking forward to a baby or not. The thought of a kid scared the shit out of me, but the idea hit me that maybe it had to do with being afraid I couldn't provide properly. As I hit Virginia I started to buy into the thought that maybe it really was the money. With the horse-track scam shut down and the cigarette scheme dwindled to a drizzle I had no way to earn. Maybe things would be all right after all since after this trip I'd start making gorilla money on the next ones.

The weather warmed as North Carolina pavement came up. I popped a cigarette between my lips and the window down. I adjusted my latest lumbar pillow and played with the radio feeling upbeat about the future. My confidence ebbed considerably when I factored in the risks I was assuming. *You moron. Why would anyone pay you ten grand if it wasn't dangerous?* This was no way to make a buck. Eventually some shit would pop up and knock me off the horse. Then what? My kid's old man would be in the big house? I slammed my hand on the steering wheel as Vinny's words haunted me about the chance to do it right with my own kid.

I exited North Carolina knowing I was back in the same old box, no way to make serious money, and no way I was going to join the zombies who did their nine-to-five bullshit.

I pulled into a rest area, hit the head and stretched before picking up a Big Mac and a double order of fries to go. The beer in the cooler was still pretty cold, and it went perfectly with the food. I leaned against the car and devoured the meal. Pulling back onto the interstate I lit a smoke and searched for a scheme.

Hitting Miami, I was down mentally but relaxed. I knew the routine now, still a chance to get rolled by the spics, but the easy part was almost over. Soon I'd be not only transporting a couple of bricks of snort but the real possibility I'd be on my way to a federal prison until I was an old man.

These guys were careful; the meet was at yet another one of the scores of Latin bars on the strip in Little Havana. At a place called The Caribe, Juan Carlos shared half a drink and set the exchange for a bakery on Seventh Street called the El Prado at 5:15 a.m.

The clock had just hit five when I rolled past El Prado. I circled around and pulled into the brightly lit lot as a dark sedan squeezed by me on the way out. *Could that have been a five o'clock exchange?*

An old man was sipping coffee and nibbling on a roll at one of the outdoor tables. He never raised his head from the paper as I swept past him into the shop. Before the door closed my contact appeared pointing to the back. I took a step forward and he shook his head, making a circle with his hand. I grabbed a hot roll off a tray, singeing my hand, took a bite and tossed it on the seat of my car as I pulled around back.

The swap took place just inside the back door. He took the cash, and I took six bricks of coke packed as loaves of bread.

Heading out of Miami, it occurred to me that huge gobs of cash were trading hands on what amounted to trust. I had no idea if the loaves were really cocaine, or fucking heroin, for that matter, but I knew the cash was real.

Chapter Thirty

We were up by three with two weeks left in the season. If we won two out of three tonight, chances were we'd lock up the prize money. Larry was a point ahead for best average but in a bad mood and bowling horribly, killing his chance to take the coveted individual crown.

After missing another easy spare in the fifth frame I pulled him aside.

"What's up, Broc?"

"Nothing."

"Bullshit, what's cooking?"

He wagged his head. "This fucking business. I can't catch a break, don't think I'm gonna make it."

"What happened?"

"Got hit with two lawsuits in the last week, and that fucking chink on Signs Road bounced a ten-grand check and is nowhere to be found."

"You'll find a way. Red. You always cry but end up on your feet."

"Not this time: behind on rent, behind on paying the crews, no fucking cash flow. My guys are leaving me." He threw up his hands. "I donno what to do. I'm thinking bankruptcy."

"You got jobs lined up?"

"Yeah, funny thing is I booked, like, five new pools but can't get the materials to build them; they cut off my credit."

"Come on, you're up again. Try and concentrate, man."

After losing two of three, barely squeaking out one game with Red throwing a gutter ball, we headed to the bar. Tommy had relentlessly busted our balls and jumped on Red for choking in the final frame. I sided up to Tommy.

"Ease up on Red. He's got a sack of shit on his plate."

He took a swig. "Join the crowd, as you would say."

I leaned in. "Just cut him some slack, all right. Looks like he's gonna lose the business."

It wasn't much of a party mood. We sucked down a few drinks, and Tommy disappeared with Larry to smoke a joint. It was getting late for those that had a regular job, so I said goodbye and stepped into the parking lot. Tommy and Red were closely huddled, talking, and when they saw me they quieted right down.

"You two staying out all night?"

"We're just bullshitting."

"Must be deep stuff, man."

They looked at each and shuffled their feet.

"What's going on?" It was apparent they were hiding something.

Tommy said, "Nothing, man, you going home, Mary?"

"Very funny, Skins." Something was up, but it'd take time to pull it from them, and I had to get up early. "I'll see you mutts around."

I felt like throwing up when I heard that Larry was arrested with a couple of kilos of coke. What the hell was going on? I couldn't believe it; it made no sense. He took stupid risks with his business, expanding like crazy, taking jobs that were way over his head, but he always busted his ass to make a buck. How did he go from hard working, albeit reckless at times, to running drugs? I had the sinking feeling that Tommy was definitely involved and recalled the night last month that Red was in the dumps, and they were huddled up in the parking lot. I felt for him, and geez, his parents. It cast a dark shadow on the neighborhood's way of life that'd be tough to get over. The distressing episode was a game changer for me, and I vowed to distance myself from my boyhood buddies.

For the second time this week, the morning meeting with Mayor Price was dominated by drug-related violence. On Tuesday, it was a drive-by shooting that killed a dealer and injured a ten-year-old girl, and last night there were three separate drug-related shootings.

Deputy Mayor Harrigan presented the daily summary finishing with, "Two victims were DOA. The third is in ICU at Mt. Sinai. They were apparently battling over territory. Just one more thing, troubling as well; there's been a steady rise in burglaries and muggings over the last ten weeks."

Mayor Price slammed a hand on the table.

"We've got to get a handle on this, and I mean now!"

"Mr. Mayor, the facts are we have the makings of a drug epidemic on our hands. Our narcotics department is reporting a dramatic decline on the street price of cocaine and heroin. There's a flood of it hitting most major cities."

"I don't give a rat's ass about any other place but New York."

"I understand, just adding color to the environment we're operating in."

The mayor waved his hand for the deputy police commissioner to continue.

"The feds are throwing more resources into interdiction, but there's a couple thousand miles of border they're responsible for."

Goldbaum jumped in. "Thank you Ray. While I appreciate the scope of the DEA's job, I share the mayor's concerns about focusing on our city. I believe we can tweak the model that worked with stemming the tide of illegal cigarettes in the city."

Harrigan snickered. "Maybe we'll even get a conviction this time."

Mayor Price glowered at his deputy and stood. "Stop bickering and get to work! All the good work I've done is not going to get tainted on my way out!"

When the mayor left, they quickly developed plans to ramp up the number of stops at all bridges and tunnels. They also agreed to study ways to limit drug-related crimes.

Goldbaum filled in his chief of staff and de facto campaign manager about the meeting.

"You know, Lew, this could be a positive for us."

"Drug-crazed killers on the streets a positive?"

"You're a prosecutor, boss; the people will look to you to get the people responsible for it."

He shook his head. "I'm in office now, and we have this problem."

"Not the same. We'll campaign on your record of convictions, your intolerance on crime. You'll shake up the police department."

"Hold on now." He threw up a hand.

"Just messaging Lew."

"Just don't trash the police, okay?"

"Sure thing."

"Look, we're going to increase the stops and seizures. I want to increase surveillance on the street dealers, put pressure at the street level, but that's going to take money and the police are over budget already."

"So? If the mayor's behind it they'll get more money."

"Gordon, fact is they've pulled money from every bucket-and-slush fund already."

Black pointed at the DA. "Why don't you fund it?"

"My office?"

"Sure, can't lose. I love it." Black got up. "We get some press that the DA is funding some of the police department's operations. If it works, you look great, and if not, you look good for doing whatever you could to protect the city."

Goldbaum stroked his chin. "I like it; call Commissioner Argento."

"Will do. Then I'll leak it." Gordon laughed as he left.

Chapter Thirty-One

I pulled up to Caesar's Lounge and went in to tell Ivan I had the Miami blow.

"Hey, Frankie, Ivan in the back?"

He nodded, "How you doing, Tommy boy?"

"Fucking beat, man," I said and walked down the hallway where Two-Ton Tony stood guard.

He threw open the door, revealing Yuri, Ivan, and Johnny One Shirt around a shot-glass-laden table with Patsy, who'd run the gambling for Louie but was now in Yuri's camp. They looked up in unison.

I threw a thumbs-up, and Ivan hopped up.

"New shirt, Johnny?" I laughed. Yuri turned his head, not even acknowledging I was there. What a prick.

Ivan jumped in my car.

"Go, make left at corner and park."

I pulled into a space about halfway on Castleton Avenue, and Ivan looked out the rear window. After five minutes, we pulled out and drove to the next block where his car was. He took the coke and sped off.

When I got to the apartment, Donna waddled over, looking more tired than me.

"Tommy, the doctor said he has to get paid before he delivers the baby."

"Hey, I'm here two minutes, and you're hounding me already?"

Her eyes watered up. "I went for my checkup, and they said we owe sixteen hundred, and if we don't…"

"Yeah? Well, fuck them. The fucking Puerto Ricans never pay."

She began to sob, and I knew if I didn't do something I'd never get to bed.

"Come on now." I embraced her. "It's gonna be okay. I'll give you the money tomorrow, okay?"

I didn't have the money, but the next trip down for Yuri would finally be a paying one. As I hit the sheets I made plans to get an advance tomorrow.

Gladiators Gym was rocking with energy. There must've been a dozen or more of Yuri's boxers training along with twenty or so gym rats. I scanned for Yuri but he wasn't there.

"Hey, Yakov, is Yuri around?"

He pointed up.

"Need to see him."

Yakov came back. "He say to wait."

There was a big bruiser banging away at the heavy bag. I watched him get instructions and pulverize the bag for ten minutes, but he was grunting so loud I went to the far corner to watch a pair of lightweights spar. After a half-dozen rounds went by with no one landing a shot of any significance I was bored. An hour had passed and I went to Yakov, who came back after checking, shaking his head no.

I left to grab a slice of pizza and came back in half an hour. Yuri's top prospect in the heavyweight class was coming out of the locker room. He was a massive Cuban who was unbeaten as an amateur. He climbed into one of the rings with his trainer. A crowd soon formed, and I was surprised at the kid's graceful ability to move around the ring.

Another hour passed—this was bullshit. I went back to Yakov. "Look, I gotta get going. I need to see Yuri; see if he's cool now."

It took ten minutes for him to wave me up.

Yuri was seated on the couch, and the TV was on.

"Yuri, I know you're busy. I just need five minutes."

"No, no busy. I watch *Dr. Zhivago*."

What the fuck? Was he pulling my leg? I glanced at the TV which had the credits rolling by.

"I need a favor."

Yuri cocked his head.

"I, you know my girl's having a baby, ready any day now. And I need an advance on the next run. The fucking doc wants to get paid before he..."

"How much?"

I pushed. "Twenty-five hundred."

He tugged his nose. "I give twenty-five. I take four K from next run."

Four thousand for like two weeks or so? "That's a bit steep, it's only for a week or two."

"You no like, go to the Bank America." He got up and sat behind his desk.

I was so thrown; I didn't know what to say or do. I looked at my watch and said, "I, I gotta run. I'll let you know."

I needed the fucking money for sure, or I'd be taking Donna to the emergency room where some fucking towel head would deliver the baby, and I'd never live it down. Since I couldn't go back to the apartment I drove to the corner of Carnegie and Richmond where Vinny's express bus stopped. He usually got home around seven. Thirty buses passed before he stepped off, suit jacket over his shoulder. I threw open a door, and he hopped in saying, "What's the matter?"

"No 'Honey, I'm home, What's for dinner?'"

I explained that I needed sixteen hundred bucks for the baby doctor. I told him the fucking Russian was trying to screw me, and as usual Vinny came through. I drove him home, and he wrote out a check that Donna would cash in the morning. Relieved, I hoped I wouldn't end up screwing him.

The news that Red was pleading guilty and would be serving at least five years in jail was difficult to deal with. A big hole in the gang suddenly colored everything. Red was one of the funniest guys on the planet, and things would never be the same. To pick up the paper and see that fucking press hound, Goldbaum, parading around like he cured cancer by jailing Broc had me boiling and feeling guilty for not somehow intervening.

Chapter Thirty-Two

When Goldbaum heard that Boris caved, agreeing to testify against Yuri Popov in exchange for immunity he called an immediate meeting. Shoulders arched back, he swept into the conference room where Turbow and Lindenberry were chatting over a cup of coffee.

"Looks like we're going to finally nail Popov," Lindenberry offered.

"There's no automatics with a jury. I, we can't tolerate a repeat with the witness."

"We've got it covered," Turbow stated.

Goldbaum beckoned with his hand. "Details Ron, details."

"Mr. Medev is in protective custody. He's in a safe house in Bay Ridge; two agents have eyeballs on him."

The DA shook his head approvingly. "Family?"

"Just a wife; she's with him."

He fished in his pocket for ChapStick. "We need to get him into witness protection?"

Lindenberry said, "He's not made it clear, worried about his businesses, doesn't want to walk away from it, seems his mother and sister in Russia are dependent on him."

"As far as his business, I'm in touch with the feds on their asset-purchase program," Turbow volunteered.

"Ron, if you need to, reach out to Flannigan. He owes me a favor or two."

Lindenberry slid a file across. "Here's his sworn statement on what he knows. He was approached personally by Popov, and when he resisted he was harassed. When we present to the grand jury we'll tag on racketeering as well."

The DA thumbed through the folder. "Have we been able to get another retailer as a witness?"

"We got a few that are willing. We'll use them, but none had direct contact with Popov. If we try, the judge will disallow it as hearsay."

"Keep digging, with Medev under lock and key we have a strong case that I'd appreciate making even stronger with another witness."

"Blake, it's Gordon. You got a few minutes for a big story?"

"On the record?"

The DA's chief of staff demurred. "Confidential. I'll give you some background, but you didn't hear it from me."

"Go ahead."

"Grand jury being convened Wednesday, solid case on a cigarette smuggling ring led by Yuri Popov."

"The Russian that slipped out of the horse racing scandal?"

"Yeah, well, you keep playing with fire, and you get burned."

"Evidence?"

"Solid firsthand witness. His testimony is going to put Popov behind bars for a long time."

"Uhm, good for the DA's mayoral gambit."

"It'd be nice to tell about the determined way DA Goldbaum has pursued and shut down the—"

"You want to write it?"

"One hand washes the other."

"Don't worry, Gordon; the DA will get his due."

The DA cringed at the *Staten Island Advance*'s page-one headline: 'Will Goldbaum Finally Get His Nemesis?'

Two thumbnail photos of the DA and Yuri appearing to look at each other sat on top of the text. Attributed to an anonymous source, the article revealed that a grand jury convening tomorrow would hear testimony and evidence to indict Yuri Popov on charges related to the smuggling of cigarettes. It alluded to the possibility Goldbaum was fixated with putting Popov behind bars because of the embarrassment he suffered in the Aqueduct case. The story mentioned Yuri's boxing gym and his many contenders, juxtaposed with the fact Goldbaum would present the case against Popov to the grand jury. The piece ended by saying that sources at the district attorney's office wouldn't confirm the target of the grand jury but didn't deny it centered on cigarette smuggling.

By Wednesday morning, every paper had a story about Goldbaum and the Popov case. As the sun peeked over the skyscrapers, Goldbaum and Turbow made the five-minute walk down to Centre Street with three briefcase-laden clerks. Turning off White Street, the DA was disappointed that the steps to the courthouse were empty and made a mental note to let his chief of staff have it. He didn't have to present the case to get an indictment, but Gordon wanted to use the opportunity for some camera time. With a full plate, he could have used the time more productively and still gotten camera time announcing the indictment.

The prosecution team entered the small courtroom spreading themselves over two tables as the court reporter emerged from the jurist entrance. As he settled behind his stenotype device he remarked to the court guard, "I thought grand jury proceedings were supposed to be secret. Silly me."

Goldbaum was about to respond when the seventeen-member panel began to enter the courtroom. He studied the mix of blue-collar workers and senior citizens as they filled the jury box and made a split-second decision as they were being sworn in. He leaned over to Turbow.

"I'll instruct the jury; you present the evidence."

With the swearing in complete, Goldbaum squared a file on the table, stood and buttoned his jacket. Eyes locked on the jury, he approached.

"Ladies and gentlemen, the oath you have taken constitutes you the grand jury for New York Superior Court. I will instruct you on your service; it is your duty to follow these instructions.

"The function of a grand jury in criminal matters is to determine whether there is sufficient evidence for an indictment against an accused. It is not your role to determine guilt or innocence.

"The guilt or innocence of a person indicted by you is determined by a trial jury. A trial jury hears all the evidence, on both sides, under the supervision of a judge. At such trial a verdict is rendered only after the defense has had an opportunity to hear the witnesses, examine the evidence, and have the case argued by their counsel.

"Your duty is only to ascertain whether there is 'probable cause.' Goldbaum fingered quotation marks. "If the evidence is sufficient to constitute 'probable cause,' then it is your duty to vote for an indictment. Probable cause is defined as a reasonable ground of suspicion, supported by circumstances strong enough to believe that this person is guilty.

"There may be instances when it seems that a crime has been committed, yet you feel that the accused is not guilty, or you have a strong doubt as to guilt. In those cases, you should vote not to indict, as you have heard only one side of the case.

"Therefore, ladies and gentlemen, when so justified it is your solemn duty to cause the accused person to be indicted; likewise, when an indictment is not justified, it is equally your solemn duty to clear the accused person."

He took a half step back and surveyed the jury. "Are these instructions clear?"

A sea of heads nodded as he moved back behind the table.

"Thank you. Assistant DA Ronald Turbow will now present the case against the accused."

Turbow scooped two files off the table and launched into his presentation.

"Ladies and gentlemen, we will show that Yuri Popov is the head of a crime organization that has engaged in the transport, sale and distribution of illegal cigarettes. In addition, he has colluded with willing retail outlets to defraud New York of millions of dollars of tax revenues. He has also engaged in criminally coercive actions to force law-abiding retailers to participate in his scheme in fear of their businesses and very lives."

He opened a file and read the list of laws that they believed were violated. Turbow passed the jury the list and followed with documentation to support the loss of tax revenues. Out of the second file he then offered the jury the scores of arrest and confiscation records he attributed to members of Popov's enterprise, followed by pictures of Yuri with some of the arrested drivers.

He collected the documentation and restuffed the files. "Copies of these will be available for your deliberative process."

Turbow went back to the table, swapped files with Goldbaum and raised his voice a notch.

"However, we believe the most damning evidence against Mr. Popov is the direct testimony of a participant in the scheme, an insider shall we say. This witness, and his testimony, is so sensitive, that he and his wife are now under protective cover."

The assistant DA put both hands on the jury rail and lowered his voice. "Out of concern for his safety, we have decided not to have him appear before you today. However, it is within your jurisdiction to compel him to appear should you wish."

He stepped back, opened the damaging file and read the sworn testimony of Boris Medev to a riveted jury.

Chapter Thirty-Three

Apsco, tipped off about the indictment before it became front page news, acted to limit the damage in the public relations arena. He advised Yuri to stay at a mutual friend's house and called the DA's office to request that a summons for an appearance be issued rather than an arrest warrant.

He suspected the DA would push for an arrest warrant but was pleasantly surprised when Lindenberry told him they'd consider it and get back to him.

Two hours later, Apsco took a call from the *New York Times* and was blindsided when asked about the arrest warrant just issued against Yuri Popov. Pissed, he advised Yuri he was sending a car for him.

Apsco then worked the phone. After venting at Lindenberry, who pleaded forgiveness as Goldbaum made the decision, he negotiated a simultaneous surrender and arraignment hearing at the district court in the morning. It ended up both Apsco and the DA got what they wanted; the agreement was essentially the same as the summons Apsco wanted, and Goldbaum had a high-profile arrest warrant. They bantered about Yuri's release after his court appearance. The DA's office mentioned the threat of Yuri fleeing and a substantial bail amount if a release was even granted. The criminal lawyer was not to be hoodwinked again and called the judge when done with Lindenberry.

"Judge Willis, sorry to disturb you, Your Honor, but I'm calling in regards to my client Yuri Popov."

"Go ahead, Counselor."

"Well, we are surrendering before you in the morning and will enter a 'not guilty' plea, but the matter of release is an important one, Your Honor."

The judge remained silent.

"We believe he should be released on his own recognizance; he has substantial business interests…"

"And how does the DA's office feel about it?"

"Frankly, Your Honor, I don't feel we can trust them."

"My, my, can't trust the DA?"

"Well, let's say that while negotiating the surrender they pulled a fast one."

"Hmm, let's see what they present in the morning. Good night, Counselor."

Yuri surrendered and was processed at the courthouse. He was the only one in the sea of orange wearing street clothes in the holding pen. When the court officer called out the docket number, Apsco rushed over as Yuri was released from the cell. They settled behind the defendants table, glancing at Lindenberry who manned the prosecution's station.

Judge Willis tapped his gavel, and the courtroom went silent as Yuri and his lawyer stood at attention. Willis read the list of charges Yuri faced and peered over his reading glasses.

"How does the defendant plead?"

"Not guilty, Your Honor." Apsco proclaimed.

Willis jotted a note as the stenographer recorded the response.

"And may we have the DA's position vis-a-vis release, bail et al."

Lindenberry scrambled to his feet.

"Your Honor, Mr. Popov is charged with a slew of serious crimes."

"The court is well aware of the charges, Mr. Lindenberry."

"Uh, yes, well, we believe the defendant is a serious flight risk. We ask that he be remanded in jail until he is tried."

"No bail?"

"Mr. Popov has considerable resources at his disposal and a release would…"

"Thank you, Mr. Lindenberry and the defenses position?"

"Your Honor, Mr. Popov has considerable business interests in New York and has close ties to the community. In fact, his pastor from St.

John's is here if you would like hear from him." Apsco waved a hand in Father George's direction."

The judge offered the priest a smile. "That won't be necessary. Continue."

"Mr. Popov has surrendered his passport already." Apsco took a step closer and lowered his voice a notch. "I'd like to note that the DA's office appears almost vindictive here. In a previous, baseless case that was dismissed, Mr. Popov made every appearance required by the court. He has demonstrated his respect of the court; therefore, if it pleases the court, we ask that Mr. Popov be released on his own recognizance."

Apsco's rear had not even hit the chair when the judge announced Yuri's release. Willis set the trial date for a mere two months away and pounded his gavel, calling for the next case.

The press had a field day with the coming trail. They rehashed the embarrassing horse racing scandal and made the new trial seem like a sporting event between two bitter rivals. Given the percentage of smokers and the cheap smokes he provided, there was a fair amount of sympathy for Yuri. It troubled the DA's campaign who worked hard to keep the crime and the negative financial impact it had on New York front and center.

As the trial neared, information began to surface about the Russian mob's involvement in the drug trade. Gordon jumped on it, planting stories connecting Yuri and his Russian crony's possible connection to help turn the public's opinion around. The last thing they needed was a win in court but a loss in Goldbaum's popularity.

On the day the trial began the *Daily News* morning paper led with the headline: 'Goldbaum Squares Off Against Popov'

It was a bold characterization but what really sold papers was the huge drawing below. It depicting Goldbaum and Yuri in opposite corners of a boxing ring with Judge Willis as referee.

The drawing reinforced the personal nature of the trial and ensured the courtroom would be packed.

When the clock struck 10 a.m., Judge Willis lumbered in, and the courtroom rose to attention. In his late sixties, the magistrate's face was heavily lined, and he favored his right leg as he climbed up to his perch. He adjusted the chair and fished out a pair of reading glasses, setting them on his capillary-filled nose. Willis knocked his gavel, rushed through the docket information and called for the prospective jurors to be brought in.

Apsco knew the case would hinge on Boris Medev's testimony and made a motion at a pretrial hearing to exclude him but had been denied. He then dug up whatever dirt there was on Medev and would do his best to discredit the witness and stunt his testimony.

When jury selection began he tried to shape the jury as best he could, stacking it with smokers and lower-class, blue-collar workers, hoping the phenomenon where the less fortunate rooted for a criminal to succeed against the system would surface. In reality, Apsco secretly thought it was the only way Yuri would walk.

Jury selection went quickly; the DA never used any of his challenges while Apsco only rejected an older white woman who'd never married.

Willis swore them in and called a recess to allow the jury to choose a foreman. He instructed them on their duties, advising that once they made their choice the trial would begin.

Goldbaum and his assistants wore navy-blue suits and white shirts. The DA completed his outfit with a red tie while Turbow and Lindenberry wore gray ones. When the jury settled into their seats, the foreman rose and identified himself to Willis, who promptly polled the jurors to be sure it was unanimous. The judge took his reading glasses off, leaned back in his chair and pointed to the prosecution.

"You have the floor."

Goldbaum rose slowly, buttoning his jacket as he came around the table. He put a hand on the table and smiled broadly.

"Ladies and gentlemen of the jury, you have been entrusted with an important responsibility."

Goldbaum took two steps toward the jury box and waved a hand across the jury. "You have the ability to make a stand against fraudulent schemes and support honest-working citizens. To signal loudly that any attempts to defraud will be met with swift condemnation." Goldbaum raised a forefinger. "This is ultimately what these proceedings boil down to; do we allow a criminal element to enrich themselves at our expense?" Goldbaum shook his head slowly and paused.

"During the course of this trial you will hear testimony, irrefutable testimony by an insider, a direct witness to the reprehensible actions of the defendant." He panned the jury box and nodded. "Yes, you will hear from an insider during these proceedings." He stepped back and crossed his arms.

"We contend that Yuri Popov and his associates, acting on his direct instruction, purchased cigarettes in North Carolina. You see, in North Carolina the tax per pack is a mere few cents versus over four dollars here in New York. They then transported them to New York, breaking several more laws on the way, where they were sold to unwitting consumers. The difference was pocketed by Mr. Popov and his cronies.

"Now this may seem enterprising and even harmless. However, let me warn you it is not." The DA pointed his finger at the jurors. "Mr. Popov has stolen from you, stolen from our children, our schools, from the firefighters and the police who protect us. He has helped widen the budget gaps that have led New York to cut services to those most in need. I tell you it is among the worst sorts of crimes as it touches each and every citizen. The damage is as widespread as any crime you could contemplate."

Goldbaum approached the jury box and put his hands on the rails. "I ask that you carefully weigh the evidence and testimony we will present against Yuri Popov. It is not a complicated case; we'll show that the defendant is the head of a criminal enterprise and not a legitimate businessman. That Mr. Popov's organization smuggled cigarettes into New York for profit. The evidence will demonstrate just how far reaching the scheme Mr. Popov ran, to defraud New York, was. You will hear how the defendant coerced individuals to participate in the fraud by having them sell the untaxed cigarettes in their stores." He stood erect and finished slowly.

"You have taken an oath that binds you to honestly consider the facts of this case. This oath gives you a responsibility to the court. But perhaps even greater, you have a responsibility to make clear that the antics of those who wish to suck the blood of our communities will be punished."

Apsco, donning a bemused look, had been shaking his head ever so slightly as the DA made his remarks. He rose from his seat and tugged at both his shirt sleeves, to be sure the right amount of sleeve showed before moving slowly to the jury box.

"Good day, ladies and gentlemen. We've heard the tale weaved somewhat eloquently by the DA." He nodded toward Goldbaum with a thin smile. "He'd have you believe that my client, businessman Yuri Popov, is the scourge of our society. That putting him behind bars would result in New York becoming a paradise. That Mr. Popov, who owns several businesses and employs scores of people, steals—that's his word—from our children, schools, firefighters, and the police. Did I leave anything out?" He smiled before adding, "Well, at least Mr. Popov is not accused of polluting our water!" The comment elicited chuckles from the jury, which the defense attorney let die down before continuing.

"The simple, though unpleasant, fact is that the DA is fixated with Mr. Popov." He put both hands on the jury rail. "I ask you to consider these facts, which are indisputable. My client came to America, legally, and worked hard to build his business interests. He has never been convicted of a crime or even a misdemeanor. I submit that this very trial is nothing more than an act of vengeance by the DA."

Judge Willis cocked his head at the stinging accusation. He seemed poised to interject but settled back in his chair.

"I'd like to paint a picture for you before we consider the flimsy evidence and hearsay that the DA will try to sell. The DA, Mr. Goldbaum, has entered the race to replace Mayor Price. He is a political animal: a publicity seeker, if you will. Why else would he be here prosecuting this, shall we say, high-profile case? I checked the record, and it is telling. Over the last four years with hundreds of cases brought and tried by his office, Mr. Goldbaum personally tried just over ten. That's right, only one or two cases a year. I'm not saying he doesn't work hard, but when he decides to appear in court, it seems to be related to how high profile the case is."

Apsco circled around and pointed at the DA. "Now let's add another fact, a very embarrassing one. There was an ill-advised attempt by the DA to connect my client to a horse racing scandal at Aqueduct. Mr. Goldbaum had an arrest warrant issued for Mr. Popov, arresting him at Madison Square Garden during a boxing match that featured one of my client's boxers. Sound a bit over the top?" He cocked his head and let it sit for second before adding, "Mr. Popov's boxer won that night in spite of the upsetting spectacle."

Apsco moved toward the defense table and swung around and raised a finger.

"Let me point out that there was no trial. Nothing happened. The DA quietly dropped the charges against my client, Yuri Popov." Apsco raised his voice. "Just quietly dropped, no press conference announcing the dropping of charges, no apology from the DA, nothing to make up for the circus-like atmosphere Mr. Popov was charged under."

Apsco hung his head. "It was a disgraceful episode in New York's judicial history. These types of witch hunts must not allowed, especially by a DA running wild in pursuit of revenge! Thank goodness the press took Mr. Goldbaum to task. The *Times* said it best, and I quote, "the best revenge is one that has gone too far!"

Apsco smiled and closed with, "In this case, ladies and gentlemen, a conviction of Mr. Popov would be going too far."

Goldbaum was smarting from the verbal attacks on his character but rationalized it proved Apsco had nothing concrete to rebut the charges. It was an attempt to distract the jury and put the focus on him rather than the defendant. He smiled at the jury, knowing he'd bring a laser-like focus to Yuri.

Judge Willis scrunched his chair up to the desk. "Counsel, please approach." Goldbaum and Apsco glanced at each other as Willis clarified. "Both of you."

Willis pushed the mic to the side. "I'd like an estimate on how long it will take each of you to present your cases."

"I, uhm, no more than a day, Your Honor. That is unless the defense, as he has been wont to do, goes crazy with crosses."

Apsco glared at Goldbaum. "Your Honor, understanding the, shall we say, thin nature of the prosecution's case, it should only take me a day to tear it to shreds."

"I'm warning both of you to keep these proceedings civil. Look, it's almost two thirty. What do you say we recess for the day, and get at it in the morning?"

The lawyers both nodded and began to walk away, when Willis said, "Mr. Goldbaum, a word please."

Goldbaum scooted back as Willis leaned over. "You're playing into his hands by making it personal. Let's keep it to the facts, shall we?"

Chapter Thirty-Four

Boris and his wife were holed up in a two-family brick home in Fort Hamilton, Brooklyn. Hiding for over ten weeks, Boris was a nervous wreck who continually fretted over his stores. Bored stiff, he took pleasure in eating and had an extra ten pounds to show for it. Though assured by the agents and his wife that after Yuri was convicted, he'd return back to the life he'd built, he didn't buy it.

As a result of his skepticism, Boris insisted on a provision that if Yuri was somehow exonerated, or if he felt threatened, he'd go in the witness program with a new identity. When the call came that he'd be testifying in the morning, Boris believed that was where they would end up.

Boris and his wife were playing Matador in the living room. Sitting on a couch; shoulders slumped more than usual over the game board, his wife asked what he wanted to order for dinner.

"Ah, my last meal on death row." He huffed.

"Oh, come now, Boris. Everything is going to work out."

"My stores, I worked like a dog to build them. Where did it get us? Now we have to run away to a new life, like criminals." He put his hand on his thinning head of hair.

"As long as we are together, that is all that matters."

He tossed a domino on the table. "And my mama? She doesn't even know where her Boris will be; maybe I will never see her again."

"Shush. Of course you will."

Agent Bruno came into the small living room, "Cheer up, Boris. It's time to eat. What do you feel like eating tonight?"

Ron Turbow stopped by with a gallon of ice cream just after dinner to check in on Boris. The assistant DA had seen many witnesses get crushed by the pressure and wanted to support him before the big day.

"Here you go, Boris, brought you something for your sweet tooth."

"Thanks."

"You feeling okay?"

"Guess so, can't wait to get this over with." Boris put his head in his hands and leaned on the sofa's arm.

"Soon, almost there."

"Maybe, but don't know how it's going to end for us."

Turbow pulled a chair in front of him and put his hands on his knees. "I talked to the DA; we made a call to the feds. We'll get you anywhere you want to go; don't you worry."

"What about my stores, my mama…"

"Easy, easy. The feds have a witness asset purchase program; you know you're not the first witness with business interests to come forward. If you feel you can't go back, for any reason—"

"What price? I worked my ass off."

"It's always been fair; we need people like you to catch the bad guys, Boris. If a price can't be agreed, they use an independent third party. I'm telling you, we got it all worked out."

"What about my mama in Russia? How will I see her? What will happen to her?"

"Have you no faith in us? When you came into custody we reached out to Interpol to alert them, and they've been monitoring the situation."

"Interpol?"

Turbow nodded. "We don't like it to get around, but in spite of whatever problems the Soviet Union and America have, the law enforcement establishment always finds a way to cooperate."

Boris brightened. "Can I tell my wife?"

"Sure, but that's it. Okay?"

"Sure, sure."

"Now remember, keep the answers short like we practiced. Just answer the questions the DA asks, don't add anything."

Boris shook his head.

"Try to look straight ahead; don't move around too much on the stand. Don't look at Popov until the DA asks you to identify him, understood?"

"Yeah, yeah, I remember."

Turbow stood and patted Boris's shoulder. "Okay, big guy, wear that nice blue suit, and remember to keep the shoulders back and smile a bit when you enter the courtroom."

Boris pulled his shoulders back. "Happy, bossman?"

Turbow chuckled. "Go have a big bowl of ice cream, and get a good night's sleep."

When morning came, the assistant DA wasn't taking any chances and arrived in an unmarked car to escort Boris to the courthouse.

The witness was hustled through a back entrance and waited on a wooden bench outside the courtroom until he was called to testify. Turbow got him a newspaper and coffee to pass the time, but Boris touched neither. The assistant DA put a hand on Boris's shoulder and gave it a quick squeeze.

"I gotta go in. You got to trust me. You do your part, and we'll do ours. Don't worry." He looked into Boris's eyes and lowered his voice. "We'll get this bastard."

A long hour passed before the heavy wooden door swung open, and a bailiff stepped into the hall.

"Mr. Medev, they're ready for you."

As Boris rose from the bench, a man dressed in a crisp gray suit appeared in the hallway. He briskly walked toward Boris, pressed a small object into his hand and disappeared. Boris looked at the vial and stopped dead in his tracks.

"You okay, Mr. Medev?" the bailiff asked.

Boris scanned the area and shook his head.

"You sure? You look pale."

He shook his head again but didn't move.

"Don't worry, everybody gets nervous when they get in the courtroom. It's natural. I see it every day."

Boris stuffed his hand and vial into a pocket and said, "Let's go."

The witness went through the door and trudged behind the bailiff to the witness stand. Though his eyes were cast at the floor, he could feel the scrutiny he was under. The courtroom clerk stopped him before he climbed onto the stand, offering a Bible. Boris placed his hand on the Bible and the clerk read the oath.

"Do you swear by Almighty God that the testimony you will give is the truth, the whole truth, and nothing but the truth."

Boris rolled his shoulder back and looked at Yuri, then the DA, whispering, "Yes."

"Be seated, please."

Goldbaum licked his lips and took a deep breath as he rose. He flashed a smile to the jury and an even broader one to the witness. The DA wore a deep blue suit, white shirt and red tie and walked stiffly in his highly polished shoes.

"Good morning, Mr. Medev. The court appreciates your appearance. Please state your full name and address for the record."

Boris didn't return the smile and leaned into a corner of his chair.

"Boris Vitaly Medev, 1401 Manor Road, Staten Island, New York."

The courtroom reporter tapped away as the DA asked, "Would you tell the court how you make your livelihood?"

Boris wore a quizzical look.

"What do you engage in to make a living, provide for your family?"

Boris straightened up. "I own two convenience stores. Bought them myself."

"Similar to 7 Elevens?"

"Well, sort of, except we don't sell dirty magazines."

Goldbaum nodded, glancing at the jury. He liked the offhand remark that strengthened his credibility.

"So, you sell a variety of goods: snacks, sodas, magazines…"

"Yes, yes, coffee, newspapers almost anything you need. You know we sell lottery tickets now."

"And what about cigarettes. Do you sell them?"

Boris slumped back. "Well, yes. It brings traffic to the store, and the customers buy other things when they come in."

"And how long have you been selling cigarettes?"

"From the beginning, as soon as we took over."

"From the moment you began to operate these stores, the first one for about eight years and the second two years ago, you've been selling cigarettes."

He nodded his head, and Goldbaum said, "Let the record reflect the witness had nodded affirmatively."

"Now, Mr. Medev, when you bought these businesses, where did you purchase your cigarettes?"

"I, uhm, well, I think the name was MJS or MSJ, something like that. They're wholesalers; they get them from the cigarette companies."

"Would that be MSJ Tobacco Products?"

Apsco, outfitted in a gray silk suit, rose to his feet. "Objection, leading the witness."

Judge Willis, hand on chin, hardly moved. "Overruled, simple clarification."

Goldbaum nodded to the judge. "Now, Mr. Medev, are you still buying from MSJ Tobacco Products?"

"No, no, we switched, got better prices from National Tobacco Wholesalers."

"I see, and did you purchase cigarettes from them all the time, from the time you changed from MSJ Tobacco until today?"

Boris frowned. "Well, you know, we made a mistake, a big mistake. I wish we hadn't done it, but we bought some cigarettes that, uhm, well, we didn't really want to do it, but…" His voice trailed off.

"Mr. Medev, did you purchase and offer for sale cigarettes that were not New York tax paid?"

Boris squirmed in his chair. "Yeah."

"How many cartons of these illegal cigarettes would you estimate were sold every month?"

"Uh, I don't know it. It varied but two thousand a month."

"Two thousand cartons, so twenty thousand packs each month. Would that be per store or combined."

"Each store."

Goldbaum turned to the jury. "That is a significant amount of taxes gone unpaid to New York, and from only two stores. Now, Mr. Medev, how did you come to purchase these illegal products?"

Boris mumbled, "Someone came to us, and we made a deal."

"As I understand it, you originally said no to buying these contraband products and were coerced into purchasing them."

"Objection, leading the witness."

Judge Willis shook his head. "Abstained."

The DA pursed his lips. "Mr. Medev, is the person you negotiated with and made an agreement to purchase these illegal cigarettes present in this courtroom?"

Boris shifted in his chair and fingered the vial in his pocket but didn't answer. Goldbaum repeated the question, and Judge Willis added, "Witness, please answer the question."

Boris stared at his lap, and Goldbaum crossed his arms.

"Mr. Medev, let me remind you that you are under oath. Now, is the person with whom you conducted your illegal cigarette activity in court today?"

Boris shook his head. "No, no."

A murmur rolled across the courtroom, and Willis lightly tapped his gavel. The DA moved a finger in his ear and cocked his head.

"Mr. Medev, perhaps you've misunderstood. Let me rephrase. The defendant, Yuri Popov, was he the one you dealt with?"

"No."

Goldbaum grabbed the file Turbow held in his outstretched arm. "Mr. Medev, let me remind you that you are under oath and can be held in contempt of court." The DA waved the file. "We have your sworn testimony attested to the fact that you personally dealt with the defendant, Yuri Popov, in conspiring to sell and profit from the sale of contraband cigarettes."

Goldbaum tossed the file back on the prosecution desk. "Now can you identify Mr. Popov as your contact in the cigarette scheme?"

Boris straightened up and looked straight at the DA. "No."

"Mr. Medev, that contradicts your sworn testimony. Are you aware that perjury is a federal offense punishable by up to five years imprisonment? I will give you one more opportunity to clarify the record."

"Objection, Your Honor. The prosecution must prove the witness is untruthful."

"I'll allow it. We do have his affidavit."

Goldbaum nodded gravely, fixing his eyes on the witness. "Boris Medev, did you purchase illegal cigarettes from Yuri Popov."

"No."

Goldbaum looked at the judge who threw him a line by tapping his gavel. "This court will be in recess until nine tomorrow morning. Counselors, my chambers please."

The DA and Apsco followed Judge Willis out of the courtroom and into a dark-paneled room. They stood before his desk as the judge took his robe off and hung it behind the door. He lowered himself into his chair and waved them into seats.

"What the hell is going on?"

"I, I believe the witness has been intimidated, tampered with."

Apsco slapped his hand on the messy desk, "This is outrageous! If the DA has any proof I suggest he provide it. Otherwise, Your Honor, I'll be filing a motion for dismissal."

Willis raised a hand. "Well, something's changed, damn it! We've got the witness's affidavit. Now it's either he's gotten cold feet or something more sinister is going on. I'll not allow my courtroom to be turned into a circus, do you hear me? Now get out of here, and figure this out—pronto!"

Apsco wore a thin smile as they both stood.

As they turned to leave, Willis said, "Louie, I'd like a word with you."

The defense lawyer left the room, and the judge spoke as he fingered a pencil.

"I don't know what's going on with your witness. I'd hate to think it's tampering." He sighed. "But this is the real world."

"Your Honor, it was a total surprise."

"And embarrassing, the press is going have a field day with this."

"We'll get to the bottom of this, I assure you."

"Be forewarned, Louie, without this witness your case is exceedingly weak. If he doesn't come around, I'll have to consider a motion to dismiss."

Boris was hustled back to the safe house where he collapsed onto a couch with his wife by his side.

Minutes later both assistant DA's stormed in and ranted, but Boris was a zombie. The frustration and screaming peaked until Boris dug out the vial and sobbed uncontrollably.

The evening's newscast covered the breaking story, and it wasn't kind to the DA's office. Local TV channels had reporters stationed at Apsco's and the DA's office, hoping to pick up insight as to why the witness clammed up. The abrupt recess fueled speculation about Goldbaum's competency and spilled into the morning papers.

The *Staten Island Advance* dedicated its entire front page to the trial, leading with a headline that shouted, "Popov Has Goldbaum on Ropes."

The *Daily News*' lead story wondered, 'Goldbaum Bumbles Again?'

And the *Times* ran a column-one story titled, 'DA Loses Another Witness?' following up on their concerns that surfaced during the Aqueduct scandal.

When Turbow and Lindenberry broke the news that Popov had gotten to Boris, Goldbaum slammed his hands on the desk and bolted up.

"Goddamn it! We can't have this thug running around making a mockery of my office. I'm going to get this bastard; he'll rot in a rat-infested jail. Why can't you get me something to hang this bastard with?"

"We thought we had it with Medev, but—"

"No butts; no more excuses! Do you realize what this makes me look like? Did you watch the news?"

They shook their heads, and Lindenberry asked, "What shall we do?" Apsco's putting a motion in to dismiss, in the morning."

The DA rambled on about moving forward without Boris Medev. He didn't have enough other evidence to convict Popov but thought he might be able to sway the jury with innuendos pointing to Popov as a witness intimidator.

"Apsco will object to anything like that, and Willis will sustain it's hearsay, inadmissible, unless we can get concrete proof, but we'd need time."

"Boss, you think we can ask the judge to suspend the trial?"

Goldbaum collapsed into his chair. "That old codger won't go along. He's a defendant's judge."

The DA dispatched Turbow to a meeting with Judge Willis and Apsco.

Willis palmed a file on his desk and looked at Turbow. "The defense has filed a motion to dismiss, and frankly, I'm looking for a reason to deny it."

"Well, Your Honor, this is a sensitive matter. The witness has been frightened. He received a vial containing what we believe is his mother's finger."

"What on earth?"

"I know, Your Honor. It's extremely troubling."

"And what does this have to do with my client?"

"Come now, Counselor. Given the reputation and history of the people you represent—"

"Your Honor, I detest taking this unfounded abuse."

Willis tapped his fingers. "Mr. Turbow, do you have any evidence vis-a-vis witness tampering?"

"Not yet."

"Any additional material evidence or witness in the case?"

Turbow shook his head.

"Well, then. I'll have to grant the motion to dismiss."

"Thank you, Your Honor." Apsco smiled at Turbow.

The judge mumbled something inaudible as he signed the motion and handed it to Apsco.

As Apsco was leaving he turned to Turbow. "Just for the record, Ron, my client has instructed me to file defamation suits against the DA, his office, et al if allegations about tampering find their way into the press."

Goldbaum met with Black in his office to discuss the damage.

"I'm not going to pull punches, Lew; this Popov mess has set us back big time."

"Tell me about it. I'm going to get this bastard, you'll see."

"Look, the calendar was blocked out with the trial and all. I thought we might use the time to hit a couple of neighborhoods, but after the last poll numbers, I'm thinking we should lie low, let a few days pass."

"You sure?"

"It's for the best. We'll keep the focus on the drug effort; go slow and rebuild your image piece by piece. It's going to be rough for a couple of days, but we keep the focus on crime. You got a couple of cases we can get in the press while Apsco has his day in the sun?"

"If we can get Popov, I'd..."

"Lew, forget him, will you?"

"But I'll get him, you wait..."

"Put him out of your head, you hear me?"

Chapter Thirty-Five

I wasn't sure taking my uncle's bread van was the right call. Every time I had a good idea to make some money, there ended up a downside. My back was aching from the cheap seat, and the pig ate gas, elevating the risk with twice as many gas ups. On the plus side, it provided cover—great cover—and I had room for a load of smokes.

The bastard Yuri didn't even give me credit when I told him I was taking the van. The idea hit me when I replayed my three runs, all with pickups at a bakery. Now with a bit of cash, I'd stop off on the way up and buy five hundred cartons. I'd lay them off without Yuri knowing; making a profit of three bucks a carton, a cool fifteen hundred.

I checked the gas gauge, just a tad over a quarter tank left. Twenty miles away to the next rest area for a fill-up and stretch. My back was killing me and I was tired. I dug the uppers out of my pocket and dropped one; it bounced off the console and disappeared. I leaned over and my back screamed, so I adjusted the crappy seat as much as I could, noting to search for the upper at the next stop.

Two stops later, I was on Route 440 heading to the Outerbridge Crossing, where the police presence was usually lighter. Making my way over the bridge, I kept pace with a UPS truck into the toll plaza where I spied a pair of cops shooting the shit through their car windows.

My eyes were glued to the toll booth, and as I paid, I noticed both cop cars pull out. I was tempted to get off at Pace Avenue, but I'd have to make an abrupt swerve. Fumbling for a cigarette, I kept in the right-hand lane as a cop pulled alongside and pointed to the shoulder. Both cars' lights advertised the stop as I took a couple of deep breaths and pulled over.

One officer came around to my side while the other, flashlight in hand, peered into the passenger cabin.

"License, registration and insurance."

"Uh, what I do, officer?" I opened the glove box and fished out the registration.

"Passenger taillight out."

"Out? I didn't know."

"Who owns the van?"

"Uh, my uncle. My aunt said it was okay to use it."

The officer checked the documents and said to his fellow officer, "Yeah, you were right; it's the truck Ruffino used."

"Where you coming from?"

"Ah, Miami, got a load of bread and pastries."

The other officer shined a light on the floor boards, "Billy, got a green pill on the passenger mat."

"What's the pill for?

"Uhm, I, I donno."

"Pick it up slowly and hand it to me."

The two officers studied the pill. "It's a greenie, an upper."

"You got a prescription for this."

"Uh, yeah. Yeah sure."

"You got it?"

"Uh, no, not on me."

"The law is they must be stowed in the bottle at all times. You have any more?"

"One or two in my pocket."

"Johnny, we have probable cause to search the vehicle."

The officer opened the driver's door saying, "Step out of the vehicle, slowly."

They asked me to turn over any other pills and made me place my hands on the hood of the car with my legs spread. The officers searched the cab but found nothing more.

"What's in the back?"

"Bread, just some bread. You know bakery stuff."

The officer took a deep sniff, looked at the other officer and said, "If that's all, then you're going be okay. Now pop the back doors."

I reluctantly opened the lock, and when the doors were opened revealing a pile of cigarettes the officers cuffed me.

"Any chance we can handle this between us?"

"You want to add attempted bribery to the list of shit you're in?"

They searched the rest of the vehicle and discovered the drugs disguised as loaves of bread.

I was shoved into the back of a cruiser and brought to a precinct. The arresting officers filled out a pile of paperwork, brought me for a mug shot and fingerprinting before I was led to be interrogated.

Lindenberry was heading out a precinct rear door as Tommy was hustled into an interrogation room. He did a double take and stepped back inside, approaching the arresting officers.

"What's up?"

"Possession of a distributable amount of cocaine, and to boot, a shitload of swag smokes."

"Nice."

"He's that mafia guy Ruffino's relative."

Lindenberry nodded. "His face looked familiar from some surveillance we did on that Russian, Popov."

"Man, isn't that guy slippery."

"I'll say."

The assistant DA stood outside the one-way window as a detective and officer questioned Tommy. He didn't have time but had an itch he needed to scratch. After ten minutes they came out of the room.

"He give you anything?"

"Nothing, another hero."

"Mind if I take a crack at him?"

"He's all yours."

"Thanks, run down the stop and arrest."

The officer gave him a summary of what led to the arrest.

Lindenberry swung the door open to the stark room, and Tommy looked up and then got back to staring at the wall as the prosecutor pulled out a plastic chair.

"I'm Assistant DA Robert Lindenberry. I'm not going to play games here, kid. You're in deep trouble."

Tommy nodded slightly.

"Like I said, I not going to dance around. I know who you work for."

"Yeah? Who's that?"

"You are part of the Ruffino crew, now run by Yuri Popov. Look, it's no secret the DA's been investigating Popov's activities for some time."

"What the fuck that got to do with me?"

"Everything to do with you if you don't want to spend the next thirty years behind bars." Lindenberry abruptly pushed his chair back. "You want to help yourself or protect Popov? It's your call. I'm going to take a leak, and when I get back you'll have your chance to help yourself if you choose. If not, I'm going home to my family."

Tommy thought of his own newborn son, pausing before responding, "What kind of help can I get?

"Depends what you give us," Lindenberry said on the way out.

The assistant DA tracked down Goldbaum at a campaign event.

"Lew, sorry to disturb you but got something that could be interesting."

"Make it quick."

"Some guy was picked up coming over the Outerbridge with cocaine and cigarettes. I was at the twenty-ninth, and he looked familiar to me from the Popov surveillance. Sure enough, he's with the Ruffino-Popov gang."

"Hmm."

"I figure with what he was transporting he's Iooking at thirty years, minimum. Maybe we can get him to open up, cut him some slack if he's willing to help us nail Popov."

"I like it; do what you need to do. Offer him whatever we need to, but it must be solid evidence."

Lindenberry took a slurp of water from the fountain before barging back into the room.

"So, what's it going to be? You going to be smart and help yourself, or play the tough guy?"

Tommy cleared his throat and offered his cuffed hands. "Wanna take these off?"

"Got to keep one on, but I'll loosen it." He smiled and adjusted the cuffs.

Tommy massaged his free wrist. "If I was to tell you some stuff, and I ain't saying I am, but like, what you do for me?"

"I spoke with DA Goldbaum a moment ago. He authorized me to negotiate a deal with you, but the information has got to be solid." He wagged a finger, sat down and said, "Look, this is dead serious, kid. You're looking at, with the new sentencing guidelines, minimum thirty years in the pen."

Tommy thrust his chin out. "So what about this deal?"

"We can be very helpful, and that's straight from the DA…"

"Helpful? What the fuck that mean?"

"Anything from say a sentence reduction, and it could be substantially shortened, to having you held in a minimum-security facility."

Tommy made a face. "Look what I know, what I can help you with is, getting that fuck head Yuri. But I can tell you, bro. If I do, and it's a big fucking *if*, I ain't spending a minute in the can."

"I don't know about that. You've committed some serious crimes."

Tommy fished a pack of cigarettes out of his pocket.

"Here, let me help you." Lindenberry tapped a cigarette out and lit it for him.

Tommy took a deep drag and blew the smoke across the table. "If I'm gonna go down this road, it's got to be the whole way. I'll deliver fucking Popov on a platter but it'll cost you cover for me, my kid, girl and mom."

"You referring to the witness protection program?

"Based on the record you guys got, I ain't going to be hanging out in the park."

"Look, it all hinges on what you can deliver on Popov and his activities."

Tommy leaned back, stared at the ceiling for a second and crushed out his cigarette. "This was my third time doing these runs down to Miami. Yuri set it up, gave me the money, and his guys took the coke."

"You dealt with Yuri Popov directly?" Lindenberry pulled out a notepad.

"Yeah, I owed him some money for gambling, and he asked me to do it to clean my slate."

"Who gave you the money?"

"Yuri."

"Where?"

"In his office, above the gym, in Heartland Village."

"How did you know who to go to make the buy?"

"Yuri set it all up and told me who and where."

"What did you do with the drugs you bought?"

"Delivered them to whoever Yuri said to."

"Was he present?"

"No, just his gorillas."

"Who told you where to bring them?"

Tommy huffed. "I told you, Yuri; I'm telling you he ran the whole shebang, man."

"What about the cigarettes?"

Tommy smiled. "Hey, that was me, figured I had the truck, was in the neighborhood. But before the cops put pressure on the smoke biz, Knob Head was knee-deep in it."

"Okay, let's stick with the narcotics charge for the moment."

Tommy looked at the wall clock. "Look, it's getting late. If I don't make the drop in an hour or two, they'll know something's gone wrong."

"Yuri going to be there?"

Tommy shrugged his shoulders. "Doubt it, but you never know."

"Hang on a minute."

Lindenberry hustled to the phone and called Goldbaum again.

"Boss, my hunch, it hit the mother lode!"

"Go on, Bob."

"He's a runner for Popov. Said he receives direct instructions from Yuri about where to make the buy and drop. Said Popov personally gives him the money for the buy. He's willing to cooperate but wants to go in the witness protection program."

"Hmm, we have to go slow, get full details. Will he wear a wire?"

"Didn't go there yet, but we got to move. He said if he doesn't make the drop in an hour or two, they'll know he got picked up."

"Can we rush a team in place?"

"Ah, I don't see how. We can have a squad car tail…"

"We need irrefutable evidence, Robert! I'm not walking into court with shit on my shoes again!"

"I, I understand, just wish we had some time to put the assets in place, get a wire and listening post up."

There was a silent pause before Goldbaum commanded. "Get a signed confessional, record it, and uhm, photograph the evidence. Then release him; let him make the drop, then get him back in this week."

"Cut him loose?"

"Yes, I'll, uh, we'll finally build a proper case on Popov."

"You sure about this?"

"You heard me. Get moving."

Lindenberry took the cuffs off, taped Tommy's waiver of counsel and details that led to his arrest. Leery, Tommy had the assistant DA, on camera, promise to drop the charges and put him in the witness protection program if he helped them in the case against Yuri Popov. Lindenberry quietly handled the paperwork, releasing Tommy and his vehicle, contraband and all.

Chapter Thirty-Six

Both hands on the wheel to steady them, I pulled out of the police station and headed to the drop site. Aware of Yuri's reach, I was afraid he'd be tipped off about my arrest. Unable to one hand my lighter, I slowed down to light a smoke and noticed a car behind with no lights on. I pulled onto Richmond Avenue. and what now looked like a tail followed. Sweat broke out on my forehead and I cranked a window. The car was two football fields behind and moving under the speed limit but I saw there were two people in it. A couple of hours ago I would be afraid it was the cops, now I could only hope it was.

As I came up to the Rockland Avenue light it turned red. I decided to run it when a tractor trailer lumbered through the intersection. I watched the tail approach, and as it came closer I realized it was just two old geezers who forgot to put their lights on. The light turned, and I headed to a shopping center just past the mall.

Everything seemed normal as I pulled past Brooklyn Bagels and went to the service entrance where a goon named Natan was just inside the door. I made the hand off and sped away. I wasn't out of the woods yet but felt relieved.

By the time I got to the apartment I was shot. My back was killing me, and I couldn't remember being this tired. I fished the key out, resolving to fall in bed immediately. The baby was crying in Donna's arms when I came in but I didn't care. I took him, kissed his cheeks and cradled him, rocking him quiet. I flopped on the couch with little Albert, and Donna snuggled up.

"You know, I didn't think it would be this good."

"I told you. You didn't have nothing to worry about. He's so cute; look at him."

I fingered his hand. "His hands, man, so teeny. Does that mean he's gonna be on the small side?"

"Don't mean nothing. You look beat."

"Yeah, running on fumes."

"Go to sleep."

"I will; anything to eat?"

"Nance brought over some sausage and peppers; I'll make you a dish."

Tommy inhaled the food, washing it down with two beers.

"You want more?"

"Nah."

"Go to bed, then."

"Uh, I got to talk with you.

"Get some sleep first."

"I gotta unload, Don. It's big."

Donna stiffened and held Albert close as her eyes moistened.

"Don't worry. It's complicated, but it's gonna be good for us, man. I'm telling you; we'll get out of this rat hole."

"What? We're we going, Tommy?"

"Almost anywhere you want."

"Thomas, stop this, and tell me what's going on."

Tommy told her he had been pinched with the bread van, leaving out the part about the drugs, and that he was asked by the DA to go into the witness program.

"But, but what would we do? How could we survive? Where would we live?"

"Look, I'll work out the details, just want you to—"

"No, I won't go! Albert is staying with me. I have my sister here."

"We got to do this, Don."

She got up. "You got yourself in the mess. I told you these frigging cigarettes were trouble. Now what? You'll get probation or something. Geez, what a disgrace. Poor Albert…"

"Sit down and shut up!" He slammed his hand on the table knocking a fork to the floor.

Donna cooed to Albert who began to cry and took a chair.

"Look, this is serious shit. I don't want no fucking lecture, you hear. Where you think this money's been coming from, huh?"

Donna shrugged.

"I was in a hole, all these expenses, the doctors and all." He hung his head a bit. "So I got a chance to make some real money, but the cargo was frigging coke."

Donna gasped. "Thomas."

"I know it was stupid, but I got nailed and bottom line is if I cooperate, they get us out of here."

Donna started to sob.

"Look it's going to be all right, going to be good, I, we get a fresh start somewhere new. We got Albert now. We'll get out of here."

"Look, we may need each other, but that don't mean I trust you guys."

Turbow countered, "It's not the way the program works. You testify, then we give the new identities and whatever cash is agreed upon."

Tommy pushed the plate of hash browns away. "I don't give a shit about any programs. You think I'm gonna let my kid and mother hang out to dry if you guys drop the ball?"

"Don't get paranoid on us, Tommy boy."

"Paranoid? No, realistic? Yes. Look, you think you know Yuri, but you don't, man. He's got a lot of people who feed him information, even the cops. Look, man, if I can't get the money and IDs for all of us, like now, I ain't doing it."

"And if you don't testify, then you realize you're going to be behind bars for a long time?"

Tommy nodded. "Yeah, but my kid, Donna, and my mother will be safe."

"Bob, you want to call Goldbaum?"

Lindenberry nodded and left the Secaucus Diner for a pay phone.

Lindenberry slid back into the booth, nodding his head. "It's a go."

Turbow cocked his head. "A go?"

"Yeah, Goldbaum said it was a special situation. We could advance the money and identities before trial. He mumbled something about a precedent…"

"All right, now one more thing."

The assistant DAs shot skeptical glances at each other and Turbow said, "What now?"

Tommy leaned back and blew a smoke ring, "Larry Broccolino, he's doing ten up in Sing Sing. You need to get him out."

"We don't have a magic wand, kid. That was a drug thing if I recall, kid pled guilty."

Lindenberry added, "I remember we had a hunch Popov was behind it, but the kid didn't give us anything." He turned to the other lawyer. "If he can back up Tommy's testimony, we could probably get it commuted."

"I don't want him involved. He has no idea I'm asking, but I got to help: he a good guy, just fucked up once, besides I'm doing enough for you guys."

"When did 'the kid plead, Ron?"

"Couple of months, tough to remember, the way time's flying."

"If it's under six months, he could file a motion to withdraw his plea and force a trial. Then we could drop it or negotiate another plea."

"I don't know. You're pushing it. We got to ask Goldbaum about this." Lindenberry looked at Tommy. "No promises. We'll talk to the DA, but the wish list is closed. Understand?"

* * *

Lindenberry and Turbow met with Goldbaum to go over the deal with their latest star witness. In return for his cooperation, Tommy, his mother, Donna and Albert would get new identities and four hundred thousand in cash. They were uncomfortable turning it over before his testimony but had to face the facts their record with witnesses was terrible. The DA glossed over the unusual accommodations and probed his assistants on the operation to ensnare Yuri. Every question received an assurance that all was under control.

"Good, good. So we're on for next Tuesday?"

"Yeah, all set. Ron's gonna be there when we kick it off."

Goldbaum nodded. "Okay thanks, gentlemen. I have to get going, another campaign stop."

"One more thing, boss.

Goldbaum eyed them.

"The witness is asking to have a friend of his released.

"Released?" The DA leaned forward onto his desk.

His assistants explained the latest request and were shocked Goldbaum quickly agreed to allow the case against Broccolino to fade away.

Chapter Thirty-Seven

Turbow took a drive to a Sayreville car wash to meet Tommy. As they watched their cars move through the building he spoke, "The thing with your friend, it's going to be handled."

"So Broc's getting out?"

Turbow nodded. "You better be sure it all goes well."

"Yeah, well, I've been thinking." He took a drag. "Four hundred K ain't enough, man."

Turbow raised an eyebrow. "Really? Poor guy, almost a half a mil, and you want more?"

"Just another two hundred, make it six hundred, okay?"

Turbow shook his head in disbelief. "Ain't going to fly, my friend. You can't keep redoing the deal."

"All I'm asking is for a measly two hundred more. We got to disappear; we'll be burning cash…"

He threw up his hand. "I'll put it to the DA, but don't get your hopes up."

When Turbow got back to the office he went to see Lindenberry.

He pulled out a chair. "You can't believe the balls on this guy."

"What now?"

"He wants another two hundred thousand."

"What? What'd you tell him?"

"Said I'd ask Goldbaum."

Lindenberry grunted. "Can't do that. He'd probably give him three hundred."

Turbow laughed. "Yeah, what's your take on it?"

They quickly agreed that not giving Tommy the extra money wouldn't derail his cooperation. They resented someone they considered a common criminal, pushing them around after they had already given him a very sweet deal. Convinced that Goldbaum would cave in his drive to put Yuri behind bars, they decided to keep the latest request secret and tell Tommy he wouldn't get a dime more.

* * *

I needed three cups of coffee to shake the lude-induced sleep out of my head. As my head cleared, uneasiness replaced it as I leaned over the crib to kiss Albert. Man, was he something! Though I knew I shouldn't, I picked him up anyway and held him tight. When I put him back down, I studied him for a few minutes. Damn, how I wished I could just hold him all day. I checked the time and looked around; the apartment suddenly looked pretty good. I shot a look at a sleeping Donna and one last one at Albert before leaving. Shitting bricks but relieved that the day had finally come, I got behind the wheel of my car.

I pulled up to an old warehouse by the water in St. George and went in to meet with the team of agents handling the surveillance. Escorted through the damp warehouse, past two undercover cars and a Con Edison van, I was shown into a trailer where four agents and Turbow were.

"You ready."

Nodding, I spit out, "Let's get this fucking thing over."

An older detective with thick glasses commanded, "Strip to the waist."

After I disrobed, he and another cop taped a transmitter into the small of my back. Then they plugged in a wire with a mic at the end and centered it on my chest.

"Move around a bit. How's it feel?"

I wiggled around. "Okay, I guess."

"Sit." The dick looked at his associate. "Okay, up. Larry, make sure it's secure."

"Didn't budge." He pointed at my clothes, and I put my shirt and jacket on.

"Let's run a test."

After confirming it worked well, the cops manning the van left to get in position, and I was given final instructions.

"Don't talk haltingly, you got to be natural. Don't slow down, it's got to be as if no one is listening, otherwise they'll be tipped off. Understand?"

"Yeah, got it."

Turbow put a hand on my shoulder. "It's going to go well. Keep your nerves in check. Get him on tape, and you'll be on a beach or wherever you're heading."

As we started out the door the older detective spoke, "Hold up there. This wire is a one-way listening device. We can't get a message to you if we see something. But if you sense something's going wrong you need to signal us."

I nodded.

"How about saying you're hungry?"

"Hungry? Yeah, that works for me."

We climbed into our cars, and the small convoy moved out.

I pulled into the Heartland Village strip mall, where Yuri had his gym, at about three in the morning. The Con Ed van was parked by a utility box in the next lot, but I couldn't pick out the unmarked cars. I went around back and was met by Ivan who ushered me up to Yuri.

The TV was on, but he must have been napping. He greeted me with a yawn.

"Ah, Tommy, this is early, no?"

"Just a bit. Gonna take a longer route, change it up some."

"You smarter than your father."

"You know, I've been thinking. To reduce the risk, why don't you make a big buy and get two, three times the amount of goods in one trip, save two, three trips."

"Less risk for driver but more risk for Yuri."

"Anyway, what am I picking up?"

He headed for the rear door of his office. "Same as before."

"So, like twenty kilos of coke?"

Yuri swung around and glared at me, putting his hand over his mouth.

As he disappeared, I whispered, "Uh, sorry."

Ten minutes later he returned with the cash stuffed in shoe boxes and handed them to me.

He turned up the TV volume and leaned in, "Islas Bakery, 137th Avenue and Thirty-Eighth Street. Okay?"

"Got it. Islas 137th and Thirty-Eighth. Now, after I give them the money, where do I bring the stash?"

He grabbed my arm, yanked me to the TV and raised the volume even higher. "Fecking shut up!"

"Okay, take it easy, man."

He released my arm. "Meet Ivan in two days: Jade Garden."

I nodded and left.

Yuri was going to go bat-shit crazy when he found out what I'd done. I was putting a ton of faith in him following the Italian code of conduct and not retaliating against my family. Hurting a woman or God forbid, a baby, was something we just didn't do. The Russians weren't so disciplined but I knew the Sicilians would stop any of Yuri's knee-jerk reactions. Plus, the cops were gonna be all over his Commie ass. My girls would be scared but okay.

* * *

Part one was over, I thought, and hopped in my car. I used the wire to advise the police that Yuri had given me the cash in shoe boxes, as I grabbed a duffel bag from the back seat. I took a long look at the cash before dumping the bundles in the bag and putting it in the passenger footwell. When I pulled onto Richmond Avenue, I spied two pairs of headlights maneuvering into position.

The roads were empty, and I sailed over the bridge onto the turnpike with my cop escort a football field away. In just over two hours I hit Delaware and pulled into a rest area to take a leak and grab a coffee. One unmarked car pulled up next to me, while the second hung on the outskirts of the exit ramp.

I grabbed the empty shoe boxes and sprung out of the car as the detective climbed out of his.

"Stopping so soon?"

"Man, I need some java and might as well take a leak."

I opened the rear door, set the boxes down and locked the door under the watchful detective's eye. He had to take a leak as well. After emptying our bladders, we grabbed coffee, gassed up and got back on the road as dawn broke.

Traffic thickened as we entered Virginia. I signaled and pulled into a busy rest area, followed by my babysitters. They went to gas up, and I got out, stretched and leaned back in the car, grabbing the duffel bag. Holding it close to my chest, I got in the morning stream of people heading to the service area. Once inside, I made a beeline to the bus ticket counter and bought two tickets, one for the commute into DC and the other to Richmond. I hurried out an opposite entrance to the bus lines and veered off to a car I had stashed in a commuter parking lot. I threw the bag in the rear, grabbed the blond wig under the seat, capped it with a Deere baseball cap and merged into the southbound traffic.

Route 66 came up within five minutes, and I headed west, sticking to the speed limit and right-hand lane for an hour and a half till the interchange for Route 81 came up. I watched my mirrors to see if anyone was following me, but couldn't detect anything.

I had to pee, but no way was I stopping. Using an old method from the cigarette-running days, I peed into an empty OJ bottle while going fifty-five miles an hour.

I pulled a pack of Marlboros and a warm Coke can out of the glove box and settled in for the southbound ride through Virginia's rolling hills. The morning radio shows dissolved into sports and church stations filled with static, so I shut it off and tried to focus on little Albert.

"What?" Lindenberry pulled the receiver from his ear. "I can't believe this shit, Ronny!"

"I know it. Unreal; he gave them the slip at a Virginia rest area."

"Nice, well, I ain't telling Goldbaum."

"Aw, come on, Bob."

"No way, man. Get someone from the OCC; get fucking Megill. It's his clowns who blew the surveillance. Let them take the heat."

Lunchtime had passed, and my stomach was aching for something more than a Slim Jim. The traffic on the now one-lane road was light as I headed deeper into rural Virginia. The gas gauge was just under half when I saw a sign for a country store. Figuring I was a half hour or more outside of Lexington I decided to stop.

I drove over gravel to the pump at Billy's Country Store, filled up and headed past a display of wooden rocking chairs to pay and grab something to eat. An old lady behind the counter didn't have provolone, so I had to settle for salami and American cheese on white bread. Grabbing a couple of bags of potato chips and a Yoo-hoo, I paid as a gray-colored cop car pulled into the lot.

The potbellied cop eyed my New York plates as I came out and turned his attention on me.

I nodded, and he said, "Looka here, a city boy at Billy's."

Trying to hide my disgust with the country bumpkin I smiled. "Not from the city, a suburb."

"Long way from home. What you doing in these parts?"

"Going rafting with some friends."

He cocked his head. "You overshoot? You're way south—"

"Coming up from Jacksonville, visiting with my grandma."

"Where you rafting?"

"Uh, it's uh, Oak Hill rafting or something like that."

He nodded, said to be careful but didn't move as I got back into my car wondering if this cop wasn't as stupid as he looked. I didn't like my gut feeling. There was a picnic bench off the gravel, and I pulled over and got out. He watched me as I sat with my food and went into the store, coming out with a cup of coffee. He waved and drove off. Forcing myself to hang, I finished my sandwich and it was a good thing. Within minutes Barney Fife had turned around, taking a long look as he drove by. I took my time, even bought another Yoo-hoo before heading west again.

I climbed a hill and passing over Clinton Forge, I could see West Virginia in the distance. I took a deep drag, tossed the butt out the window and smiled. *Maybe It's going to work after all.* The smirk disappeared as I thought of my new son. I felt I was doing the right thing for him and Donna and hoped I'd be able to keep doing the right thing.

After spending two hours winding north, I pulled into a cheap motel in the rafting town of Oak Hill. We'd gone rafting on the Cheat River as teenagers, and I knew I could hide out for a few days as just another guy going rafting. I paid cash and stuck to my room, went over my plans and dreamed of how I'd spend the money on things for Albert. As the fourth morning broke, and rafters began to assemble in the parking lot, I hopped in the car and drove off, anxious to be reunited with Albert and Donna.

As the signs for Ohio came up, I started to feel good, patting myself on the back for the plan I'd made. I hit Route 70 and got into the stream of traffic heading north to Akron. The afternoon began to fade as I headed west to Toledo and the last of the day's light disappeared north on Route 75 enroute to Michigan.

About five minutes outside of Detroit's Ambassador Bridge, I paid cash for a room at a Red Roof Inn. I grabbed a disappointing bite at an IHOP, watched TV and tried to get some sleep.

Up at five, I dressed, stuffing most of the cash in my jacket and pants and then surveyed the parking lot. I walked a few cars down to a black Eldorado, looked around and swiped its Canadian plates. My plate screws preloosened, it took mere seconds to swap plates. I got behind the wheel, shoved my NY plates under the seat and headed to the border.

Lines of trucks and cars commuting to jobs had already formed at the bridge. Two lanes of traffic crawled over the bridge, spilling into a Canadian processing plaza. The plaza had five toll-like lanes that were manned and two others blocked with orange cones. I was behind a blue Impala with Michigan plates in a line of about fifty cars until the booths. I fiddled with the radio and smoked a couple of cigarettes as the line inched along.

When I was about ten cars away an officer appeared walking past the cones in the closed lane to my left. He stopped a car away, pointed at me and motioned me into the closed lane. My heart sank as my respect for the DA's office soared. They weren't a bunch of morons after all.

Chapter Thirty-Eight

Assistant DA Turbow and Johnny Megill, the chief of organized crime control, delivered the stunning news to Goldbaum. The district attorney pursed his lips but said nothing. He rose slowly from his chair, finally speaking in a restrained manner.

"Disappointing, gentlemen. Deeply disappointing." He crinkled his brow and sat back down, forcing the chair to roll back.

Megill cleared his throat. "I'm as disappointed as you are; these guys should have known better. They're veterans for Chrissake."

"Yeah, well, they acted like goddamn rookies, letting him out of their sight? You can't make this shit up."

Goldbaum pushed him palm forward. "May I assume we are doing all we can to, ah, retrieve him?"

The chief replied, "I got three additional details already down there, and we've got an all-points bulletin for Virginia, PA, Delaware…"

"We must be careful here." The DA got up and closed the blinds. "No leaks about this. Am I clear?"

"Sure but…"

Goldbaum glared. "No buts, no excuses, no more cock-ups! This is a disgrace! If the press gets wind of this, they'll make us out to be clowns. So, keep it quiet. Understood?"

His visitors nodded.

"Now, where do we think he's headed?"

* * *

Apsco was tipped off about Tommy's disappearance before Goldbaum was told but kept Yuri in the dark. He didn't want his client sending another posse on the hunt. As far as he was concerned the best thing for Yuri's case would be for the critical witness to vanish permanently. As the central evidence in the case, their inability to present his direct testimony would have the added benefit of the jury seeing how dysfunctional the prosecutors were. Apsco could taste another victory over Goldbaum and knew this would be the sweetest yet.

Shitting enough bricks to build a bank, I sucked my chest in and zipped up my jacket. I quickly made sure no bulges were showing and pulled into the empty lane. Two uniformed officers were by the booth as sweat dripped from my underarms. I was tempted to hit the gas as I approached the booth, when an agent removed the orange cone and spoke, "Passport."

I held my breath and brought the bogus Canadian document I'd paid for into view, but instead of taking the passport he waved me through. I was stunned, pausing as the officer said, "Let's get a move on; everyone wants to get to work."

Glancing in the rearview mirror, I saw a long line of cars behind me, realizing I was just the first car in a lane that just opened. Pulling away, I unzipped my jacket and tried to unglue the sweat-soaked shirt from my back.

I'd never been north of the border, a little too cold for my blood, and was edgy as I closed in on my goal.

It was a straight run into Toronto on a truck-filled, six-lane pipeline. In just under five hours the skyline of the city, punctuated by a needle-like building, appeared on the horizon. Anxious to dump the car, I headed to the airport. I parked in a long-term lot, transferred the cash into the duffel bag and took a shuttle bus to the terminal where I rode a courtesy bus to a Days Inn.

In the morning, I hopped off the shuttle bus at Toronto Airport and headed to Air Canada's display board. Checking the departure times for international flights, I focused on countries in the British Commonwealth. Canada was a member, and other members hardly ever gave each other's citizens a hard time, I was told. I zeroed in on England, the British Virgin Islands, and even Australia and New Zealand—anywhere but India. If something went wrong as I made my way to Italy, I wasn't going spend any time in one of their prisons.

London sounded good, but the main thing was getting out of Canada. I focused on the daily flights for London, Tortola, and as an outside shot, Sydney. Checking the times for flights to Montreal, I bought a ticket for a departure leaving an hour before the London flight. Then I bought some duty-free goods and headed for the gate.

The London gate area was half full, and I scanned the waiting passengers. I spent almost an hour making my decision and with fifteen minutes before the Montreal flight was to begin boarding, made my move.

I plopped down with my bags next to a twentysomething-year-old who nodded in acknowledgment, then went back to his car magazine.

"You traveling alone, like me?"

He said, "Yeah, my dad lives in London."

I extended my hand. "My name's Jacob."

"Paul. Nice to meet you, Jacob."

"Parents split?"

He nodded.

"Me too. I know the drill, man. It's a bitch."

"Yeah, been like two years since he moved."

"If they don't get along, it's probably better. When my dad moved out my mom adjusted. She did well till he died."

"Sorry to hear."

"Well, anyway, now I'm in the same boat."

"What do you mean?"

"Well, you see, me and my wife, we split up, but she's coming after me, wants every penny I got."

"They can do that?"

"Yeah, well, she caught me with another chick, and my lawyer says the judge is gonna crush me."

"Oh boy, that sucks."

"Tell me about it. That's why I'm taking off."

"You're running away?"

I put my finger to my lips and leaned in. "Look, you want to make a quick two thousand dollars?"

He moved back. "I, I don't want to get involved, sorry."

"Listen. It's easy." I pulled out my boarding pass for Montreal. "I'll give you this, and you take this flight to Montreal. Just give me your ticket for this London flight, and I'll give you two grand, cash."

"I donno about this. I could get in trouble…"

"What trouble? You just took a flight to Montreal."

"My dad's expecting me though."

"Tell him you didn't feel good, and you'll leave tomorrow."

"But I'd have to get another ticket. I paid for it, and my bags are checked and…"

I leaned in and fanned a wad of cash. "Look, here's five grand, man. It'll cover your tickets with a ton to spare. Don't worry about your bags; the airline will hold them."

He stared straight ahead.

"Come on, man. You'd be helping me out and making easy money. What'd you say?"

"Can you make it six thousand?"

"Let's move it. the Montreal flight is boarding."

I pressed the cash in his hand and grabbed his ticket as we hustled to the gate. I hung to make sure the plane was in the air, then scooted back to board the London flight. Shit, this was easy, I thought as I settled into row twenty-eight.

I had trouble staying awake as the ferry to Calais France made its way across the English Channel and was fast asleep when we docked. I wished I either hadn't drunk so much on the flight or had a greenie to keep me awake. As I walked off the ferry, the thought of contacting my family gave me a boost.

I changed some cash into francs and bought a calling card. It took me six tries to get an operator who spoke enough English on the pay phone, and I had to repeat the number of a distant Italian cousin three times before I was connected and passed a message.

Ten minutes late the pay phone jingled, and Donna's sweet voice nearly brought me to tears.

"How you doing? How's my boy?"

"Oh, Tommy…" Donna sobbed.

"Ahem, cool it."

"Okay, okay. Yeah, yeah. He's doing great, misses you though."

"Soon enough, baby. Soon enough."

"I miss you so much."

"It's going to work out. Finally, it's going to work out for us."

"You think so?"

"Damn right. Look, we got to be careful here. I'll call in a couple of days."

* * *

Using Eurail to move into Italy was another good idea. I had been against trains, but my Sicilian contacts were right; it was filled with tourists, and no document checks were made at crossings. I was met in the Cinque Terre area and given Italian identity papers by a quiet man called Caserto. After I handed over twenty thousand dollars we headed for Rome.

Arriving at the giant rail terminal in Rome, Caserto handed me off to a close friend of my mother's sister. Gianfranco had a bushy moustache and gold front tooth that glinted in the sun. A pleasant, laid-back man, he drove like a lunatic, while speaking good English nonstop.

I clung to the door handle as we made the five-hour drive to an area called Puglia. We headed south on roads lined with cypress trees, to the heel of Italy, into the seaside resort area of Brindisi. It was nearing the end of the tourist season, and after we feasted on seafood I was given a room in the small hotel, Amatobene. Between the wine and traveling, I collapsed on the bed, wriggled out of my wrinkled clothes and slept like little Albert.

In the morning Gianfranco collected his thirty grand fee and took me for a skimpy breakfast and some shopping. Pushing me into clothes I'd never wear in New York, he helped me to blend in. Then he took me to two restaurants, introducing me to the families that owned them and told me I was safe with them. Afterward, we walked down to the tourist-filled promenade where Gianfranco told three cafés that I was an old family friend staying in town for a few weeks and was on his tab.

Over a two-hour lunch on the shimmering Adriatic Sea, Gianfranco reminded me to lay low and that he'd be back at the end of the season and take me to a place called Alberrobello, where I'd wait out the winter.

A tourist destination, Brindisi was a good place to hide, and I felt that the money I'd spent to disappear was well worth it. I made sure to run and swim to combat the wine, food and boredom as the days melted away. In a sort of paradise but isolated I was thankful when my bushy-mustached contact arrived back in town.

We piled into his Fiat Avanti and headed for Alberrobello. Gianfranco described it as a cozy town of stone-domed homes that were rented for the summer, but because they had no heat, lay empty for five months in winter. Gianfranco said he'd gotten it stocked up with provisions, including a cassette tape course on Italian, to last the winter and that when spring came I'd be able to go to Sicily.

The curvy streets were desolate, and we winded our way through town, stopping at a circular, stone house with a cone roof. He showed me around what was basically a one-room hut and handed me a number to reach him in case of an emergency. Gianfranco reminded me to keep to myself, practice my Italian and stay in the house as much as possible. Then he gave me a Beretta pistol, kissed me on both cheeks and melted away.

Alone, the months dragged on. Cooking, keeping warm and practicing my Italian only ate up a tiny part of the day, so to keep from going stir crazy in the damp hut, I drank a ton of wine and slept. Keeping limited to a measly call every three weeks to my family was tough. Hearing my son babbling did nothing but anger me. I was missing seeing him grow and vowed to make up for lost time.

Spring began to show its presence and my impatience. Then on a bright morning I heard Gianfranco's Fiat slide to a halt outside the door. Now I knew how the guys who did time felt like. I gathered my things, and we left for Sicily.

I never felt better being reunited with my family. Unsure whether it was the relief from running or a change in me, I reveled in their presence. The weeks passed into months, and slowly we altered our routines from strolls on quiet beaches and cafés in small town squares to going out in plain sight. Sicily just felt safe. The people were tight, and outsiders, meaning anything but an Italian, weren't welcome.

Alberto flourished, but I was worried he'd become just a little too Italian for me. Donna and my mother were content in the simpler life the island ran on, but I wasn't totally sold. One thing was sure was that the money I had left went a heck of a lot further than it did in New York, and that took some pressure off. All in all, though I got bored often, I thought I was pretty happy.

Mom watched Alberto as Donna and I went with a cousin, just back from New York, for drinks at a night club on the Ionian Sea. We had a good time and headed home at three in the morning. I saw Donna in, then told her I was going to town to make a call.

The doors of the elevator opened on eleven and I exited, balancing my *Daily News*, bagel and coffee. I called out good mornings as I made my way to the new fax machine. I grabbed the curly papers that came in overnight, tucked them under my arm and went to my department.

Sorting the faxes as I sipped coffee, the switchboard operator buzzed.

"Vinny, you have a call on twenty-three, a Mr. Otis from The Skins Company."

I broke into a wide smile and grabbed the receiver.

The End

I hope you enjoyed reading this book as much as I enjoyed writing it. If you did, I'd appreciate it if you would write a quick review on Amazon or your favorite book site. Reviews are an author's best friend, and even a quick line or two is helpful. Thanks, Dan.

You can keep abreast of my writing and have access to free and discounted books by joining my newsletter. It comes out just once a month and also contains articles on self-esteem, motivational pieces and pieces on wine. It's free. www.danpetrosini.com

Other Books by Dan

Luca Mystery Series

Am I the Killer—Book 1
Vanished—Book 2
The Serenity Murder—Book 3
Third Chances—Book 4
A Cold, Hard Case—Book 5
Cop or Killer?—Book 6
Silencing Salter—Book 7
A Killer Missteps—Book 8
Uncertain Stakes—Book 9
The Grandpa Killer—Book 10
Dangerous Revenge—Book 11
Where Are They—Book 12

Suspenseful Secrets

Cory's Dilemma—Book 1

Other works by Dan Petrosini

The Final Enemy
Complicit Witness
Push Back
Ambition Cliff

Manufactured by Amazon.ca
Bolton, ON